The Lost Tiger

Akshya Kumar Jal

Published by Akshya Kumar Jal, 2024.

This is a work of fiction. Similarities to real people, places, or events are entirely coincidental.

THE LOST TIGER

First edition. October 12, 2024.

Written by Akshya Kumar Jal.

Table of Contents

BOOK INTRODUCTION :

In a world where screens dominate our lives, have you ever wondered what would happen if the knowledge gleaned from endless hours of television viewing could actually save a life? "The Lost Tiger" takes you on an extraordinary journey that challenges the notion of wasted time and redefines the meaning of heroism in the most unexpected way.

This captivating tale follows Ravi, a young man dismissed by his family as a lazy, unambitious couch potato, whose life takes a dramatic turn when his successful older brother is kidnapped. As the family descends into panic and despair, Ravi makes the shocking decision to embark on a rescue mission, armed with nothing but his wits and the surprising wealth of knowledge he has accumulated from countless hours of watching television.

What sets "The Lost Tiger" apart is its unique exploration of the hidden potential within those often labeled as underachievers. It challenges our preconceptions about the value of different forms of learning and experience, suggesting that even seemingly frivolous pursuits can yield unexpected benefits. Through Ravi's incredible adventure, readers are invited to reconsider their own judgments about productivity, ambition, and the diverse ways in which people can contribute to the world around them.

The book delves into several key themes that resonate with readers of all backgrounds. First and foremost, it examines the concept of personal growth and self-discovery. As Ravi faces increasingly daunting challenges in his quest to save his brother, he uncovers strengths and abilities he never knew he possessed. This journey of self-realization serves as an inspiring reminder that we are all capable of more than we might believe.

Another central theme is the power of unconventional knowledge. In a society that often prioritizes traditional academic learning, "The Lost Tiger" makes a compelling case for the value of diverse information sources. Ravi's ability to apply lessons from survival shows, weather documentaries, and even heist movies to real-world situations challenges readers to reconsider the potential applications of their own eclectic knowledge bases.

Family dynamics and the impact of expectations form another crucial theme throughout the narrative. The stark contrast between Ravi and his successful older brother, coupled with his family's initial skepticism about his abilities, highlights the often damaging effects of familial pressure and stereotyping. As the story unfolds, readers witness the transformation of these relationships, emphasizing the importance of looking beyond surface judgments and recognizing the unique strengths of each individual.

The book also explores the theme of resilience in the face of adversity. Ravi's journey is fraught with physical dangers, emotional setbacks, and moments of self-doubt. Yet, his perseverance and ability to adapt and learn from each challenge showcase the incredible resilience of the human spirit. This aspect of the story serves as an inspiration for readers facing their own obstacles, encouraging them to push beyond their perceived limitations.

Lastly, "The Lost Tiger" delves into the complex relationship between virtual experiences and real-world applications. In an age where concerns about screen time and digital detachment are prevalent, this narrative offers a nuanced perspective on how media consumption can, in some cases, prepare us for real-life challenges in unexpected ways.

While "The Lost Tiger" appeals to a broad audience, it holds particular relevance for young adults and anyone who has ever felt underestimated or misunderstood. The book speaks directly to those who may not fit conventional molds of success, offering a powerful message about the diverse paths to personal achievement and societal contribution. Additionally, parents, educators, and mentors will find valuable insights into nurturing and recognizing potential in unexpected places.

Readers of "The Lost Tiger" will gain a fresh perspective on the nature of intelligence and capability. The book challenges the notion that there is only one path to success or one definition of a meaningful life. Through Ravi's journey, readers are encouraged to reflect on their own hidden talents and the potential applications of their unique knowledge bases, regardless of their origins.

Moreover, the book offers practical lessons in problem-solving and adaptability. As Ravi applies his unconventional knowledge to overcome each obstacle, readers are inspired to think creatively and draw connections between seemingly unrelated areas of knowledge. This approach to problem-solving can be invaluable in both personal and professional contexts, fostering innovation and resilience in the face of challenges.

"The Lost Tiger" also provides a poignant exploration of family dynamics and personal growth. Readers will gain insights into the impact of familial expectations and the importance of looking beyond initial impressions. The evolving relationships between Ravi, his brother, and the rest of his family offer valuable lessons in communication, understanding, and the power of support and belief in one another.

Furthermore, the book serves as a testament to the importance of perseverance and self-belief. Ravi's journey from self-doubt to confidence is both inspiring and instructive, offering readers a roadmap for overcoming their own insecurities and pushing beyond their comfort zones. This aspect of the story is particularly relevant in today's world, where self-doubt and imposter syndrome are common experiences for many.

The narrative also provides a unique perspective on the value of media literacy and critical thinking. As Ravi navigates his adventure using knowledge gained from various television programs, readers are encouraged to consider how they consume and process information from different sources. This aspect of the book promotes a more thoughtful and analytical approach to media consumption, a crucial skill in our information-saturated age.

In addition, "The Lost Tiger" offers a nuanced look at the concept of heroism. By presenting a protagonist who doesn't fit the traditional mold of a hero, the book expands our understanding of what it means to be brave, resourceful, and impactful. This redefinition of heroism can be empowering for readers who may not see themselves reflected in conventional heroic narratives.

The book also touches on themes of cultural understanding and the dangers of stereotyping. Through Ravi's interactions with local allies and his navigation of unfamiliar environments, readers are prompted to reflect on their own preconceptions and the importance of open-mindedness in cross-cultural encounters.

Readers will gain a deeper appreciation for the natural world and the challenges of survival in harsh environments. The vivid descriptions of the jungle setting and the various obstacles Ravi faces serve as a reminder of the power and unpredictability of nature, fostering a sense of respect and wonder for the natural world.

Moreover, "The Lost Tiger" provides valuable insights into the psychology of kidnapping and the impact of such traumatic events on families. While the narrative maintains an overall tone of adventure and personal growth, it doesn't shy away from exploring the emotional toll of the kidnapping on Ravi, his brother, and their family. This aspect of the book can be particularly enlightening for readers interested in psychology, family dynamics, or crisis management.

The book also offers a unique perspective on the concept of intelligence and learning styles. By showcasing how Ravi's unconventional knowledge proves crucial in a life-or-death situation, "The Lost Tiger" challenges traditional notions of intelligence and education. This can be particularly validating for readers who may excel in areas outside of traditional academic measures, encouraging them to recognize and value their unique cognitive strengths.

In terms of personal development, readers will find numerous takeaways from Ravi's journey. The story serves as a powerful reminder of the importance of stepping out of one's comfort zone, facing fears, and embracing new challenges. Ravi's transformation from a passive observer to an active participant in his own life story can inspire readers to take more initiative in pursuing their goals and dreams.

The book also provides an interesting commentary on the role of technology and media in our lives. While it acknowledges the potential drawbacks of excessive screen time, it also presents a balanced view by showcasing how media consumption can, in some cases, provide valuable knowledge and skills. This nuanced approach can help readers reflect on their own relationship with technology and consider ways to engage with media more mindfully and productively.

Furthermore, "The Lost Tiger" offers insights into the nature of courage and bravery. Ravi's journey demonstrates that true courage isn't about the absence of fear, but rather the willingness to act despite it. This portrayal of bravery as a conscious choice rather than an innate trait can be empowering for readers facing their own challenges.

The narrative also touches on themes of forgiveness and reconciliation, particularly in the context of family relationships. As Ravi's family comes to recognize and appreciate his unique strengths, readers are prompted to consider the importance of forgiveness, understanding, and the ability to revise one's opinions of others.

Readers will also gain a deeper understanding of the psychological impact of being underestimated or dismissed by others. Ravi's initial lack of confidence and his subsequent growth offer valuable insights into the effects of low expectations and the transformative power of believing in oneself. This aspect of the story can be particularly resonant for anyone who has struggled with self-doubt or felt overlooked by others.

The book also provides an interesting exploration of the concept of practical intelligence versus academic intelligence. Ravi's ability to apply theoretical knowledge to real-world situations highlights the importance of not just acquiring information, but also understanding how to use it effectively. This can be a valuable lesson for readers in both educational and professional contexts.

Moreover, "The Lost Tiger" offers a unique perspective on the nature of adventure and personal growth. It suggests that transformative experiences don't always require exotic locations or extraordinary circumstances – sometimes, the most profound journeys of self-discovery can begin right in our own living rooms. This idea can be particularly encouraging for readers who may feel limited by their circumstances or resources.

The narrative also touches on themes of sacrifice and prioritization. As Ravi embarks on his rescue mission, he is forced to leave behind his comfortable life and face numerous hardships. This aspect of the story prompts readers to reflect on what they would be willing to sacrifice for their loved ones or for a greater cause, encouraging a deeper consideration of personal values and priorities.

In addition, the book provides valuable lessons in resourcefulness and adaptability. Ravi's ability to improvise solutions using limited resources and to quickly adapt to changing circumstances is both impressive and instructive. These skills are increasingly valuable in our rapidly changing world, and readers can draw inspiration from Ravi's approach to problem-solving.

"The Lost Tiger" also offers an intriguing commentary on the nature of preparation and readiness. While Ravi's television-based knowledge might seem trivial at first, it ultimately proves to be crucial to his survival and success. This serves as a reminder that we can never truly predict which skills or knowledge might prove useful in the future, encouraging readers to approach all learning opportunities with an open mind.

Furthermore, the book provides insights into the dynamics of teamwork and collaboration. As Ravi joins forces with unexpected allies and eventually works together with his brother, readers are reminded of the power of cooperation and the importance of recognizing and leveraging diverse strengths within a team.

The narrative also explores the concept of identity and self-perception. Ravi's journey forces him to confront and ultimately redefine his own self-image, moving from seeing himself as a passive observer to recognizing his potential as a capable and resourceful individual. This transformation can inspire readers to examine and challenge their own self-perceptions and the labels others might have placed on them.

Readers will also gain insights into the nature of fear and courage. As Ravi faces numerous dangerous situations, the book provides a nuanced exploration of how fear can be both a hindering force and a survival mechanism. The narrative demonstrates how courage often involves acknowledging and working through fear rather than its absence.

Moreover, "The Lost Tiger" offers a unique perspective on the value of empathy and understanding. As Ravi navigates unfamiliar territories and interacts with diverse characters, his ability to empathize and connect with others proves crucial to his success. This aspect of the story highlights the importance of emotional intelligence and cross-cultural understanding in our increasingly interconnected world.

The book also provides an interesting commentary on the nature of success and achievement. By presenting a protagonist who finds his strength in unconventional ways, it challenges readers to reconsider their definitions of success and to recognize the diverse paths one can take to make a meaningful impact.

In essence, "The Lost Tiger" is more than just an adventure story – it's a powerful exploration of human potential, the value of diverse knowledge, and the transformative power of believing in oneself. As you embark on this journey with Ravi, prepare to be entertained, inspired, and perhaps even challenged to reconsider your own hidden strengths and untapped potential. Who knows? The next time you find yourself absorbed in a television show, you might just be preparing for your own extraordinary adventure.

Chapter 1: The Couch Potato

Ravi Singh was, by all accounts, a creature of habit. Every day, without fail, he would wake up at the crack of noon, shuffle his way to the living room, and plop himself down on the worn-out couch that had long since molded itself to the contours of his body. The television, his constant companion, would flicker to life with a soft hum, bathing the dimly lit room in a kaleidoscope of colors and sounds. This was Ravi's world, a carefully curated realm of sitcoms, documentaries, and reality shows that provided him with an endless stream of vicarious experiences.

As the afternoon sun struggled to penetrate the heavy curtains, Ravi's mother, Priya, would invariably peek into the room, her face a mixture of concern and exasperation. "Ravi, beta," she would sigh, "don't you think it's time you did something with your life?" Her words would hang in the air, competing with the laugh track of whatever show currently held Ravi's attention. He would mumble a non-committal response, his eyes never leaving the screen, as his mother retreated, shaking her head in disappointment.

To the Singh family, Ravi had become something of an enigma. At 25 years old, he was the youngest of three siblings, and by far the least ambitious. His days were a blur of channel surfing and snack consumption, punctuated only by the occasional bathroom break or reluctant appearance at the dinner table. His father, Rajesh, a successful businessman, had long since given up on trying to motivate his youngest son. "Some people are just not cut out for the real world," he would often remark to his wife, loud enough for Ravi to hear from his perch on the couch.

The contrast between Ravi and his older brother, Vikram, could not have been starker. Vikram was the pride of the Singh family, a rising star in the corporate world with a corner office and a string of accolades to his name. He was everything Ravi was not - ambitious, driven, and successful. Family gatherings were often dominated by tales of Vikram's latest achievements, while Ravi sat silently, picking at his food and longing for the comfort of his beloved television.

Yet, beneath the surface of Ravi's seemingly lethargic exterior, there was more than met the eye. As he absorbed show after show, his mind was quietly cataloging a vast array of information. From survival techniques gleaned from rugged adventurers braving the wilderness to intricate plots of crime dramas, Ravi's brain was a repository of knowledge that spanned the spectrum of human experience - all filtered through the lens of television.

His family, however, remained oblivious to this hidden depth. To them, Ravi's TV habit was nothing more than a waste of time, a symptom of his lack of direction and purpose. They couldn't see that with every documentary he watched, every reality show he analyzed, Ravi was unknowingly preparing himself for an adventure that would challenge everything they thought they knew about him.

As the days blended into weeks and months, Ravi's routine remained unchanged. He became an expert at tuning out the disappointed sighs and pointed comments from his family members. His world was contained within the flickering screen before him, a window to experiences and places he never dreamed of encountering in real life. Little did he know that fate had other plans, plans that would soon drag him out of his comfort zone and into a reality more challenging and thrilling than any TV show could ever be.

The Singh household had settled into an uneasy acceptance of Ravi's lifestyle. His parents had all but given up on seeing him make something of himself, instead focusing their pride and attention on Vikram's continued success. Ravi's sister, Anjali, who was married and lived in another city, would occasionally call to check on him, her voice tinged with a mixture of concern and resignation. "Are you still watching TV all day, Ravi?" she would ask, already knowing the answer. Ravi would mumble an affirmative, his attention divided between her voice and the program he was watching.

Despite the family's perception of him as lazy and unambitious, Ravi didn't see himself that way. In his mind, he was a student of life, albeit one who preferred to study from the comfort of his living room. He absorbed information like a sponge, his brain a treasure trove of trivia and knowledge gleaned from countless hours of television viewing. He could recite obscure facts about ancient civilizations, explain complex scientific theories, and even speak a smattering of foreign phrases picked up from international dramas.

But this knowledge remained locked away, hidden behind Ravi's quiet exterior and apparent lack of motivation. His family never thought to engage him in conversation about the shows he watched, assuming they were all mindless entertainment. If they had, they might have been surprised by the depth of his understanding and the breadth of his knowledge.

As another day drew to a close, Ravi found himself engrossed in a documentary about tigers in the Indian jungle. The majestic creatures moved with grace and power across the screen, their striped coats gleaming in the dappled sunlight filtering through the dense foliage. The narrator's voice painted a vivid picture of the challenges these animals faced in the wild, from habitat loss to poaching. Ravi leaned forward, captivated by the story unfolding before him.

Little did he know that this particular show would soon take on a significance beyond mere entertainment. The knowledge he was absorbing about the Indian jungle, its inhabitants, and the challenges of survival in such an environment would prove crucial in the adventure that lay ahead. But for now, Ravi remained blissfully unaware of the impending upheaval in his life, content in his role as the family's resident couch potato.

As the credits rolled on the tiger documentary, Ravi stretched and yawned, his muscles stiff from hours of inactivity. He glanced at the clock, realizing it was well past midnight. The house was quiet, his parents long since retired to bed. In these late hours, Ravi often felt a fleeting sense of guilt about his lifestyle, a nagging feeling that perhaps his family's assessment of him wasn't entirely unfair. But these moments of introspection were quickly pushed aside, buried beneath the comfort of routine and the promise of another day filled with televisual escapism.

He shuffled to the kitchen, opening the refrigerator door and basking in its cool glow as he contemplated a midnight snack. As he reached for a leftover container, his eyes fell on a framed photo magnetized to the fridge door. It was a family portrait from a few years ago, taken at Vikram's graduation ceremony. Ravi stared at his own image in the photo, barely recognizing the young man with the awkward smile and ill-fitting suit. Has he really changed so much? Or had he simply retreated further into himself, finding solace in the predictable world of television rather than facing the uncertainties of real life?

Ravi shook off these uncomfortable thoughts, grabbing his snack and heading back to the living room. As he settled back onto the couch, he flipped through channels, looking for something to distract him from his momentary bout of self-reflection. He finally settled on a late-night talk show, allowing the host's jovial banter to wash over him like a soothing balm.

As Ravi drifted off to sleep, the TV still flickering in the darkened room, he had no idea that his life was about to change dramatically. The couch potato was about to be uprooted, thrust into a real-life adventure that would test every ounce of the knowledge he had accumulated through his countless hours of TV watching. The coming days would challenge not only Ravi's perception of himself but also his family's long-held beliefs about his capabilities and character.

For now, though, Ravi slept peacefully, his dreams a jumble of tiger stripes and jungle landscapes, blissfully unaware of the pivotal role he would soon play in a drama far more intense and personal than anything he had ever witnessed on his beloved television screen.

Chapter 2: A Brother's Disappearance

As the sun rose over the bustling city of Mumbai, casting long shadows across the cramped apartment complexes, the Kumar family's world was about to be turned upside down. The previous chapter had introduced us to Ravi, the family's perceived black sheep, content with his life as a couch potato. But now, as we delve into the heart of this gripping tale, we witness the moment that would catapult Ravi from his comfortable cocoon into a world of danger and self-discovery.

The day began like any other in the Kumar household. Mrs. Kumar was in the kitchen, the aroma of freshly brewed chai and spicy samosas filling the air. Mr. Kumar sat at the dining table, his nose buried in the morning newspaper, occasionally muttering about the state of politics. Ravi, true to form, was sprawled on the couch, remote in hand, flipping through channels with the practiced ease of a seasoned TV enthusiast. The only absence was that of Vikram, Ravi's older brother, who had left early for work at his prestigious law firm.

It was the shrill ring of the landline that shattered the morning's peaceful routine. Mrs. Kumar wiped her hands on her apron and hurried to answer it, expecting perhaps a call from a relative or a telemarketer. But as she listened, her face drained of color, and the receiver slipped from her trembling fingers, clattering to the floor.

"Amma? What's wrong?" Ravi called out, momentarily tearing his eyes away from the television. The look of sheer terror on his mother's face made him sit up straight, a knot of dread forming in his stomach.

Mrs. Kumar's voice quavered as she spoke, her words barely above a whisper. "It's Vikram. He's... he's been kidnapped."

The news hit the family like a physical blow. Mr. Kumar leapt from his chair, sending it crashing to the floor. "What? How? When?" he demanded, his voice a mix of disbelief and mounting panic.

As Mrs. Kumar relayed the scant details provided by the caller - a member of Vikram's law firm - the reality of the situation began to sink in. Vikram had never made it to work that morning. His car had been found abandoned on a lonely stretch of road leading out of the city, with signs of a struggle evident. A crude ransom note had been left on the driver's seat, demanding an exorbitant sum for Vikram's safe return.

The once-orderly apartment descended into chaos. Mrs. Kumar collapsed into a chair, her sobs echoing through the small space. Mr. Kumar paced furiously, alternating between muttering prayers and cursing the kidnappers. And Ravi, for once, found himself completely ignored as his parents grappled with the horrifying news.

In the midst of the turmoil, Ravi felt as though he were watching a scene from one of his beloved TV dramas unfold before his eyes. But this was no scripted show with a guaranteed happy ending. This was real, raw, and terrifying. His brother - the golden child, the successful lawyer, the pride of the family - was in danger. The thought sent a chill down Ravi's spine.

As the initial shock began to subside, practical concerns started to surface. Mr. Kumar, his voice hoarse with emotion, began making frantic phone calls to the police, to Vikram's colleagues, to anyone who might be able to help. Mrs. Kumar, her hands shaking, tried to piece together Vikram's last known movements, searching for any clue that might lead them to her beloved son.

Ravi, still rooted to the couch, found himself struggling to process the situation. Vikram had always seemed invincible to him - smart, successful, and capable. The idea that someone could overpower him, could snatch him away in broad daylight, seemed impossible. Yet the evidence was undeniable.

As the day wore on, the apartment became a hub of activity. Police officers came and went, their faces grim as they took statements and examined photographs of Vikram. Family friends and relatives poured in, offering support and sharing in the family's distress. Through it all, Ravi remained on the periphery, watching and listening, his mind racing with thoughts he couldn't quite articulate.

It was late in the evening when Inspector Sharma, the lead investigator on the case, pulled Mr. and Mrs. Kumar aside for a private conversation. Ravi, his curiosity piqued, edged closer to eavesdropping.

"Mr. and Mrs. Kumar," Inspector Sharma began, his voice low and serious, "I won't sugarcoat this. Your son's kidnapping appears to be professionally executed. We believe it may be connected to a case he was working on - a high-profile corporate lawsuit with significant stakes."

Mrs. Kumar gasped, her hand flying to her mouth. Mr. Kumar's face hardened. "Are you saying this isn't just about ransom?" he asked, his voice tight with anger and fear.

Inspector Sharma nodded grimly. "It's a possibility we have to consider. The ransom demand may be a smokescreen for something more complex. We're exploring all angles, but I must warn you - this could be a long and difficult process."

As Ravi absorbed this information, a strange feeling began to stir within him. For the first time in his life, he felt a burning desire to do something more than just watch from the sidelines. His brother was in danger, possibly because of his work, his dedication to justice. The thought of Vikram facing this alone, while they all sat helplessly at home, was unbearable.

That night, as the Kumar household finally fell into an uneasy silence, Ravi lay awake in his bed, staring at the ceiling. The events of the day played on repeat in his mind, like one of his favorite shows stuck on a loop. But this was no entertainment - this was his family's reality now.

As he tossed and turned, unable to find rest, Ravi's thoughts turned to the countless crime dramas and action movies he had watched over the years. He had always viewed them as mere entertainment, a way to escape the monotony of his daily life. But now, in the face of this very real crisis, he found himself wondering - could any of that knowledge be useful? Could he, Ravi the couch potato, possibly have something to contribute to finding his brother?

The idea seemed absurd at first. He was no hero, no detective, no action star. He was just Ravi, the family disappointment, the one who had never lived up to expectations. And yet, as the night wore on and sleep continued to elude him, the seed of an idea began to take root in his mind.

What if he could use what he knew? What if all those hours in front of the TV hadn't been wasted after all? What if Ravi Kumar could be the one to save his brother?

As the first light of dawn began to creep through his window, Ravi made a decision that would change his life forever. He would not sit idly by while his brother's fate hung in the balance. He would act, he would search, he would do whatever it took to bring Vikram home.

Little did Ravi know that this decision would lead him on an adventure beyond his wildest imagination, testing every ounce of his courage and ingenuity. As he finally drifted off to sleep, exhausted but determined, the stage was set for an unlikely hero to emerge from the most unexpected of places.

In the coming days, as the police investigation stalled and the family's hopes began to dim, Ravi would find himself stepping up in ways no one - least of all himself - could have predicted. The journey ahead would be fraught with danger, filled with challenges that would push him to his limits and beyond. But for now, as Mumbai awakened to another day, the transformation of Ravi Kumar from couch potato to reluctant hero was just beginning.

As we leave the Kumar family in this moment of crisis, we can't help but wonder: What will Ravi's next move be? How will he begin his quest to save his brother? And most importantly, can a lifetime of watching television truly prepare him for the real-world challenges that lie ahead? These questions and more will be answered as we move forward into the next chapter of our story, where Ravi must confront his own doubts and his family's skepticism to become the hero his brother desperately needs.

Chapter 3: The Reluctant Hero

As we move from the shocking news of Ravi's brother's kidnapping, we find ourselves at a pivotal moment in our protagonist's journey. The family's world has been turned upside down, and amidst the chaos and despair, an unlikely hero emerges from the depths of the living room couch.

Ravi, the perennial couch potato, surprises everyone – including himself – by making the audacious decision to rescue his brother. It's a moment that defies all expectations, shattering the image of the lazy, unmotivated young man that his family had grown accustomed to. The very notion of Ravi embarking on such a dangerous mission seems almost comical to those who know him best.

As news of Ravi's intentions spreads through the household, the reactions are a mix of disbelief, concern, and barely concealed skepticism. His parents exchange worried glances, their faces etched with lines of anxiety. They struggle to reconcile the image of their TV-addicted son with the determined young man standing before them, declaring his intent to venture into the unknown.

"But Ravi," his mother protests, her voice quavering with emotion, "you've never even been camping! How do you expect to survive in the jungle?" Her words hang in the air, heavy with the weight of years of low expectations.

Ravi's father, a man of few words, simply shakes his head in disbelief. His silence speaks volumes, conveying a mixture of concern for both his sons and doubt about Ravi's capabilities. The family's skepticism is palpable, a tangible force that threatens to smother Ravi's newfound resolve.

Yet, something has changed within Ravi. The news of his brother's kidnapping has awakened a dormant part of his psyche, igniting a fire that not even he knew existed. As he stands before his doubting family, there's a glint in his eye that speaks of determination and a hint of defiance.

"I know what you all think of me," Ravi says, his voice steady despite the trembling in his hands. "But I'm more than just a guy who watches TV all day. I can do this. I have to do this."

The family's reaction is a stark reminder of how Ravi has been perceived all these years. Their doubt serves as both a challenge and a motivation, fueling his determination to prove them wrong. At this moment, Ravi is not just fighting to save his brother, but also to redefine himself in the eyes of those who matter most to him.

As the reality of Ravi's decision sinks in, the family's skepticism begins to mingle with a reluctant admiration for his courage. They may doubt his abilities, but they cannot deny the bravery it takes to volunteer for such a perilous mission. This conflicting emotion creates a palpable tension in the household, as they grapple with their concern for both sons and their surprise at Ravi's unexpected show of bravery.

In the days that follow, Ravi throws himself into preparation with an intensity that shocks his family. Gone are the endless hours of mindless TV watching. Instead, Ravi is a man on a mission, driven by a purpose that transforms him before their very eyes.

What his family doesn't know, however, is the secret source of Ravi's newfound knowledge and confidence. In the privacy of his room, Ravi begins to draw upon an unexpected well of information – the countless hours of television he has consumed over the years. Shows that were once merely entertainment now become valuable resources in his quest to save his brother.

Survival shows, nature documentaries, and even action movies take on new significance as Ravi mentally catalogs useful information. He recalls episodes of "Man vs. Wild" where Bear Grylls demonstrated how to find water in the wilderness, how to create shelter from natural materials, and how to navigate using the stars. Discovery Channel documentaries about jungle ecosystems suddenly become crucial study material.

Ravi's preparation goes beyond mere theoretical knowledge. He begins to practice knot-tying techniques he learned from a sailing documentary, perfecting the art of creating secure shelters and rappelling ropes. He studies maps of the region where his brother was last seen, correlating the information with geographical insights gleaned from travel shows.

Even his extensive viewing of crime dramas proves unexpectedly useful, as Ravi applies deductive reasoning techniques to analyze the limited information they have about the kidnapping. He creates a makeshift investigation board in his room, connecting pieces of information with strings, much like the detectives he's watched on screen.

As Ravi immerses himself in this unorthodox training regimen, a transformation begins to take place. The slouched posture of the couch potato gives way to a more alert, focused demeanor. His eyes, once glazed over from hours of passive viewing, now shine with purpose and determination.

This change doesn't go unnoticed by his family. They watch with a mixture of surprise and growing respect as Ravi dedicates himself to his mission. His mother, initially the most vocal in her doubts, finds herself torn between concern for his safety and pride in his newfound drive.

"I've never seen him like this," she confides to her husband one evening, her voice a mixture of worry and wonder. "It's like he's become a different person overnight."

Ravi's father, traditionally a man of few words, finds himself at a loss to describe the transformation he's witnessing in his son. He observes Ravi's preparations with a growing sense of admiration, though his concern for both his sons prevents him from fully embracing Ravi's plan.

As the day of Ravi's departure approaches, the atmosphere in the house is charged with a complex mix of emotions. Fear for the safety of both brothers mingles with a grudging hope inspired by Ravi's determination. The family's perception of Ravi is undergoing a seismic shift, though doubt still lingers beneath the surface.

On the eve of his journey, Ravi stands before his assembled family. Gone is the slouching, unmotivated young man they once knew. In his place stands a determined individual, his backpack filled with carefully chosen supplies, his mind brimming with knowledge gleaned from years of television viewing.

"I know you're worried," Ravi addresses his family, his voice steady despite the gravity of the situation. "I know you think I can't do this. But I've learned more than you realize from all those shows I've watched. Every documentary, every survival show, every crime drama – they've all prepared me for this moment. I'm not just going in blind. I have a plan, and I will bring my brother home."

The conviction in Ravi's voice gives his family pause. For the first time, they begin to see him not as the lazy son who wasted his days in front of the TV, but as a resourceful individual who has found an unconventional way to prepare himself for an extraordinary challenge.

As Ravi prepares to step out into the unknown, he carries with him not only the hopes of his family but also the weight of his own transformation. He is no longer just Ravi the couch potato, but Ravi the reluctant hero, embarking on a journey that will test everything he has learned from his years of television watching.

The coming days will prove whether Ravi's unorthodox preparation will be enough to face the real-world challenges that await him in the jungle. As he takes his first steps towards rescuing his brother, Ravi is not just venturing into the wild – he's stepping into a new version of himself, one that even he is just beginning to understand.

As Ravi disappears into the early morning mist, his family watches with a mixture of fear and newfound respect. They are left to ponder the transformation they've witnessed and to hope that the unexpected hero they've discovered in their midst will be enough to bring both their sons home safely.

With Ravi's departure, the stage is set for an adventure that will test not only his physical endurance and survival skills but also the practical application of knowledge gained from years of passive viewing. As we follow Ravi into the unknown, we stand on the brink of discovering whether a lifetime of watching television can truly prepare someone for the challenges of the real world.

Chapter 4: Into the Unknown

As Ravi stepped into the dense foliage of the jungle, the weight of his decision pressed heavily upon him. The cool morning air carried the scent of damp earth and exotic flora, a stark contrast to the familiar aroma of his living room couch. The rustling leaves and distant animal calls replaced the comforting hum of his television, and for a moment, Ravi felt a pang of regret. But the image of his brother, somewhere in this vast expanse of green, steeled his resolve.

The first few hours of his journey were marked by an awkward dance with nature. Ravi's feet, accustomed to the soft carpet of his home, now stumbled over gnarled roots and slippery stones. Each step was a reminder of how ill-prepared he was for this adventure. Yet, as he pushed deeper into the jungle, a strange sense of familiarity began to creep in. The dense canopy above, the winding paths below – it all seemed eerily reminiscent of countless episodes of "Man vs. Wild" he had binge-watched over the years.

As the sun climbed higher in the sky, casting dappled shadows through the leaves, Ravi found himself facing his first real challenge. A wide, swift-flowing river cut across his path, its waters churning with an ominous energy. For a moment, panic threatened to overwhelm him. But then, like a beacon of hope, a memory surfaced – Bear Grylls, the intrepid host of "Man vs. Wild," crossing a similar river using a makeshift raft.

With trembling hands but growing determination, Ravi began to gather fallen logs and vines. His movements, initially clumsy, gradually became more purposeful as muscle memory from hours of watching survival techniques kicked in. As he lashed the logs together, Ravi couldn't help but chuckle at the absurdity of his situation. Here he was, the family's designated couch potato, channeling the spirit of a seasoned adventurer.

The raft, crude but functional, bobbed precariously as Ravi pushed it into the water. With each stroke of his improvised paddle, a mix of fear and exhilaration coursed through his veins. The roar of the river filled his ears, drowning out the doubts that had plagued him since leaving home. As he reached the opposite bank, soaked but triumphant, Ravi felt a surge of confidence. Perhaps he wasn't as helpless as everyone, including himself, had believed.

As the day wore on, Ravi faced a series of challenges that would have seemed insurmountable just hours earlier. A steep cliff face loomed before him, its jagged surface a daunting obstacle. But instead of despair, Ravi felt a spark of recognition. He recalled an episode where the importance of testing each handhold was emphasized. Slowly, methodically, he began his ascent, his fingers seeking out sturdy grips, his feet finding purchase on narrow ledges.

The physical exertion was unlike anything Ravi had experienced before. His muscles screamed in protest, sweat stung his eyes, and his breath came in ragged gasps. Yet with each foot of progress, a strange sense of elation grew within him. This was a real, tangible achievement – far removed from the passive consumption of his TV-watching days.

As he reached the top of the cliff, Ravi allowed himself a moment of rest. Gazing out over the vast expanse of jungle stretching to the horizon, he was struck by a profound realization. The world beyond his television screen was infinitely more complex, more challenging, and more rewarding than he had ever imagined. The thought of his brother, lost somewhere in this green maze, no longer filled him with just fear, but also with a fierce determination.

The fading light brought new concerns. Night in the jungle, Ravi knew from countless documentaries, was a different beast altogether. As darkness began to creep in, the sounds of the forest changed, taking on a more ominous tone. Ravi's mind raced, recalling episodes about jungle survival after dark. He needed shelter, and he needed it fast.

With efficiency that surprised even himself, Ravi began to construct a lean-to shelter. His hands, soft from years of holding remote controls, now worked with unexpected dexterity, weaving branches and leaves into a sturdy structure. As he gathered dry tinder for a fire, Ravi found himself muttering instructions he had heard countless times on screen. "Always keep your fire small and controlled," he whispered, a wry smile playing on his lips at the absurdity of talking to himself in the middle of the jungle.

As the small fire crackled to life, casting flickering shadows on the surrounding foliage, Ravi allowed himself to reflect on the day's events. He had faced challenges he never thought possible, drawing on knowledge he hadn't realized he possessed. The image of his family's skeptical faces flashed in his mind, and for the first time, he felt a twinge of something akin to pride.

Yet, as the night deepened and unfamiliar sounds echoed through the darkness, doubt began to creep back in. Was he truly capable of finding and rescuing his brother? Or was this all a fool's errand, destined to end in failure? Ravi huddled closer to his fire, its warmth a poor substitute for the comfort of home.

In the flickering firelight, Ravi's mind wandered to his brother. Where was he now? Was he safe? The enormity of his task suddenly felt overwhelming. But then, unbidden, came memories of the countless heroes he had watched on screen – ordinary people facing extraordinary circumstances and emerging victorious. If they could do it, why couldn't he?

As exhaustion finally overtook him, Ravi's last conscious thoughts were of the journey ahead. Tomorrow would bring new challenges, new fears to overcome. But it would also bring him one step closer to his brother. With that thought, Ravi drifted into an uneasy sleep, the sounds of the jungle a constant reminder of the unknown world he had entered.

The first light of dawn found Ravi already awake, his body stiff from the unfamiliar sleeping arrangements but his mind surprisingly alert. As he doused the remnants of his fire and dismantled his shelter, leaving no trace of his presence as he had learned from countless nature documentaries, Ravi felt a new sense of purpose. The jungle, which had seemed so alien and threatening the day before, now felt almost familiar.

Setting off into the green expanse, Ravi's steps were more confident, his eyes keener as they scanned the environment for signs of his brother's passage. He found himself automatically cataloging plants that could be useful, identifying bird calls, and noting the direction of water sources. It was as if years of passive observation had suddenly crystallized into practical knowledge.

As the morning wore on, Ravi encountered a patch of dense undergrowth, seemingly impenetrable. For a moment, he hesitated, the old Ravi threatening to resurface with doubts and fears. But then, almost instinctively, he reached for a sturdy branch, recalling a technique he had seen for navigating thick jungle terrain. With each swing of his makeshift machete, Ravi felt a surge of empowerment. He was no longer just a spectator; he was an active participant in his own adventure.

The heat of the day brought new challenges. As sweat poured down his face and his throat parched with thirst, Ravi found himself longing for the air-conditioned comfort of his living room. But then, like a lifeline, he remembered an episode about finding water in the wild.

With renewed energy, he began searching for the telltale signs of hidden water sources.

When he finally stumbled upon a small stream, its water clear and inviting, Ravi felt a rush of gratitude for all those hours spent glued to the television. As he cupped his hands to drink, after carefully purifying the water using techniques he had learned, Ravi marveled at how his perceived weakness – his TV addiction – had become his greatest strength in this unfamiliar world.

As the day progressed, Ravi's journey took him through a myriad of terrains, each presenting its own set of challenges. A treacherous ravine required all his newly acquired skills to navigate safely. An encounter with a group of curious monkeys tested his knowledge of wildlife behavior. With each obstacle overcome, Ravi's confidence grew, along with a deepening respect for the complexity and beauty of the natural world.

As the sun began its descent, painting the sky in hues of orange and pink, Ravi found a suitable spot to make camp for the night. His movements were more assured now, the process of setting up shelter and starting a fire almost second nature. As he sat by the flickering flames, preparing a meal from edible plants he had gathered throughout the day, Ravi reflected on how much he had changed in just two days.

The Ravi who had left home seemed like a distant memory – a pale shadow compared to the person he was becoming. Yet, as night fell and the jungle came alive with nocturnal sounds, thoughts of his brother and the dangers he might be facing kept Ravi from feeling too self-congratulatory. His journey was far from over, and the greatest challenges likely still lay ahead.

As he settled in for the night, his makeshift bed far more comfortable than it had been the previous evening, Ravi's mind turned to what the next day might bring. The unknown, which had once filled him with paralyzing fear, now held a sense of anticipation. Whatever challenges awaited him, Ravi felt ready to face them, armed with his unlikely but invaluable TV-gained knowledge and a newfound belief in himself.

With the sounds of the jungle as his lullaby, Ravi drifted off to sleep, his dreams a mix of television adventures and his own real-life experiences. Tomorrow would bring him closer to his goal, closer to his brother, and closer to discovering just how much he was truly capable of achieving.

As dawn broke on the third day of Ravi's journey, the jungle seemed to come alive with new vigor. The chorus of bird calls and the rustle of awakening creatures created a symphony that was both alien and oddly comforting to Ravi. As he packed up his camp and prepared to set out, he couldn't help but feel a sense of belonging in this wild place that he had never experienced in the confines of his home.

The day ahead promised new challenges and discoveries, but Ravi felt ready to face them. With each step deeper into the unknown, he was not just searching for his brother, but also uncovering hidden depths within himself. The couch potato was transforming, shedding his old skin like the snakes he had watched so many times on nature documentaries.

As Ravi set off, his movements fluid and purposeful, he couldn't help but wonder what new trials and triumphs awaited him in the depths of the jungle. The thought both thrilled and terrified him, but one thing was certain – he was no longer the same person who had reluctantly left home just days ago. With renewed determination, Ravi pressed on, ready to face whatever the jungle had in store for him.

Chapter 5: Jungle Trials

As Ravi ventured deeper into the dense jungle, the reality of his situation began to sink in. The lush greenery that had seemed so inviting from the safety of his living room now loomed ominously around him. The chirping of exotic birds and the rustling of unseen creatures created a cacophony that both thrilled and terrified him. This was no longer the comfortable world of his beloved nature documentaries; this was real, raw, and potentially dangerous.

As the day wore on, Ravi found himself facing his first major obstacle. Before him lay a wide, fast-flowing river, its waters churning with a ferocity that made his heart race. The bridge that he had hoped to find, based on his rudimentary map, was nowhere in sight. Panic began to set in as he realized that this was not a challenge he could simply switch off or fast-forward through. This was real life, and he was alone.

For a moment, Ravi felt the weight of his family's skepticism bearing down on him. He could almost hear his father's voice, laced with disappointment, "What did you expect, Ravi? Life isn't like your TV shows." But then, as if on cue, a memory flickered in his mind. It was an episode of "Survival Experts" he had watched just a few weeks ago. The host, a grizzled outdoorsman with a penchant for dramatic narration, had demonstrated how to cross a similar river using a makeshift raft.

With renewed determination, Ravi set about gathering fallen logs and vines. His hands, soft from years of wielding nothing more strenuous than a remote control, soon became raw and blistered. But he persevered, recalling the precise knots and lashings he had seen on the show. As he worked, a small smile played on his lips. Who would have thought that all those hours of TV watching would actually come in handy?

After what seemed like hours of labor, Ravi stood back to admire his handiwork. The raft was far from perfect – it was lopsided and looked about as sturdy as a house of cards – but it was his creation. Taking a deep breath, he pushed it into the water and clambered aboard. The raft dipped alarmingly under his weight, and for a heart-stopping moment, Ravi thought it would capsize. But it held, and with a mixture of relief and pride, he began to paddle across the surging river.

As he fought against the current, using a long branch as a makeshift oar, Ravi couldn't help but laugh at the absurdity of his situation. Here he was, Ravi the couch potato, navigating a treacherous river in the middle of a jungle. If only his family could see him now. The thought gave him strength, and with each stroke, he felt a growing confidence in his abilities.

Halfway across the river, disaster struck. A hidden rock tore a hole in his raft, and water began to seep in at an alarming rate. Panic threatened to overwhelm him, but once again, Ravi's TV knowledge came to his rescue. He remembered an episode of "MacGyver" where the resourceful hero had patched a leaking boat with chewing gum and a candy wrapper. While Ravi had neither of those items, he did have his waterproof jacket. Without hesitation, he stripped it off and used it to plug the hole, securing it with vines.

The makeshift repair held, and with a final burst of effort, Ravi guided his battered raft to the opposite shore. As he dragged himself onto dry land, exhausted but exhilarated, he realized that he had done more than just cross a river. He had crossed a personal Rubicon. For the first time in his life, Ravi felt truly capable, truly alive.

As night began to fall, Ravi set about making camp. Once again, his TV-watching habits proved invaluable. He constructed a lean-to shelter using techniques he had seen on "Wilderness Survival," and even managed to start a small fire using the friction method he had observed countless times on various shows. As he sat by the flickering flames, warming his hands and drying his clothes, Ravi reflected on the day's events.

He had faced a significant challenge and overcome it through ingenuity and perseverance. The realization filled him with a warm glow of pride. Perhaps his family had been too quick to judge him. Perhaps there was more to Ravi than met the eye. As he gazed into the fire, he found himself looking forward to the challenges that lay ahead. For the first time, he felt equal to them.

The next morning dawned bright and clear, finding Ravi already awake and eager to continue his journey. As he packed up his meager belongings, he noticed something that made his heart skip a beat. There, in the soft mud by the river's edge, were footprints. Human footprints. And they were fresh.

Excitement surged through Ravi. Could these be traces of his brother's kidnappers? Or perhaps even his brother himself? With renewed energy, he set off following the tracks, his senses heightened and alert. The jungle seemed less intimidating now, more like a puzzle to be solved than an overwhelming obstacle.

As he trekked through the dense foliage, Ravi's mind raced with possibilities. He recalled an episode of "CSI: Jungle Edition" (a show he had always considered a bit far-fetched) where the investigators had used subtle clues in footprints to deduce information about the people who had left them. Scrutinizing the tracks before him, Ravi noticed that they were deeper on one side, suggesting that whoever had made them was carrying a heavy load.

His brother? Or perhaps something valuable that the kidnappers were transporting? Either way, Ravi felt he was on the right track. The thought spurred him on, pushing him to move faster, climb higher, and push through the fatigue that was beginning to set in.

As the day wore on, Ravi encountered more challenges. A steep cliff face blocked his path, forcing him to recall rock climbing techniques he had seen on "Extreme Sports Weekly." His hands, already sore from building the raft, screamed in protest as he hauled himself up the jagged surface. But with each painful inch gained, Ravi felt his confidence grow. He was no longer just surviving; he was thriving.

At the top of the cliff, Ravi paused to catch his breath and survey his surroundings. The view was breathtaking, the jungle stretching out before him like a vast green ocean. For a moment, he forgot about his mission, lost in the sheer beauty of the wilderness. It was a view no TV screen could ever truly capture, and Ravi felt a pang of regret for all the real-world experiences he had missed while glued to his couch.

But there was no time for regrets now. As Ravi scanned the horizon, something caught his eye. In the distance, barely visible through the trees, was a plume of smoke. His heart raced. Where there was smoke, there were people. And where there were people in this remote jungle, there might be answers about his brother's whereabouts.

With renewed determination, Ravi set off towards the smoke. The going was tough, the jungle seeming to grow denser with each step. Thorny vines snagged at his clothes, and hidden roots threatened to trip him at every turn. But Ravi pressed on, drawing on reserves of strength he never knew he possessed.

As he neared the source of the smoke, Ravi's steps became more cautious. He recalled episodes of "Spy Games" and "Covert Ops," where the heroes would stealthily approach enemy camps. Crouching low and moving slowly, Ravi edged closer, his heart pounding so loudly he was sure it would give him away.

Finally, through a gap in the foliage, Ravi caught sight of a small clearing. In it stood a rudimentary camp – a few tents, a smoldering fire, and most importantly, people. Rough-looking men moved about the camp, their voices low and their movements purposeful. With a jolt, Ravi realized he was looking at his brother's kidnappers.

For a moment, fear threatened to overwhelm him. What was he thinking? He was no hero, no trained operative. He was just Ravi, the TV addict who had never faced real danger in his life. But then, unbidden, came the memory of his brother's kindness, of the unwavering belief his brother had always had in him, even when everyone else had written Ravi off as a lost cause.

Drawing a deep breath, Ravi steeled himself. He might not be a real-life action hero, but he had something those kidnappers didn't expect – a lifetime of vicarious experiences gleaned from countless hours of television. As he settled in to observe the camp and plan his next move, Ravi felt a strange calm descend over him. He was no longer just watching an adventure unfold on a screen; he was living it. And somehow, against all odds, he felt ready for whatever came next.

As the day progressed into evening, Ravi continued his careful surveillance of the kidnappers' camp. He meticulously noted their routines, the changing of guards, and the layout of the tents. His mind, usually filled with trivia from game shows and plot twists from dramas, was now solely focused on formulating a rescue plan.

In the fading light, Ravi spotted a familiar figure being led from one of the tents – his brother. The sight of his sibling, looking haggard but alive, sent a surge of emotions through Ravi. Relief, anger, and determination all mingled together, strengthening his resolve. He had come this far; he would not fail now.

As night fell, Ravi retreated to a safe distance to rest and strategize. He knew that attempting a rescue in the dark would be foolhardy. Instead, he spent the night rehearsing various scenarios in his mind, drawing inspiration from every heist movie and spy thriller he had ever watched. By dawn, he had a plan – risky and far-fetched, perhaps, but it was all he had.

With the first light of day, Ravi set his plan in motion. Using skills he had learned from a survival show, he fashioned crude traps from vines and branches, setting them up along the paths leading away from the camp. These wouldn't stop the kidnappers, but they might slow them down in case of a pursuit.

Next came the most daring part of his plan. Recalling a technique from a nature documentary about primates, Ravi began to move through the trees surrounding the camp. It was terrifying at first, each creak of a branch sending his heart racing. But as he progressed, he found a certain rhythm to it, his body adapting to this new mode of travel with surprising ease.

From his elevated position, Ravi was able to get a better view of the camp's layout. He spotted his brother, now tied to a tree at the edge of the clearing. Two guards stood nearby, looking bored and inattentive. This was his chance.

Using a bird call he had learned from a birdwatching program (who knew that would ever come in handy?), Ravi managed to draw the attention of the guards. As they peered into the jungle, trying to spot the source of the unusual sound, Ravi made his move. Swinging down from the trees with a grace that would have shocked his family, he landed silently behind his brother.

"Ravi?" his brother whispered, disbelief evident in his voice. "Is that really you?"

"Shh," Ravi hushed him, working quickly to undo the ropes. "We don't have much time."

Just as the last knot came free, one of the guards turned back. His shout of alarm rang through the camp, and suddenly, chaos erupted. Ravi grabbed his brother's hand and ran, his heart pounding in his ears. They crashed through the undergrowth, the angry yells of the kidnappers close behind them.

As they ran, Ravi's traps began to pay off. He heard curses and thuds as their pursuers fell victim to his handiwork. But they couldn't rely on that for long. They needed to disappear.

Remembering an episode of "Manhunt," Ravi led them to a nearby stream. "We need to wade through the water," he explained breathlessly to his confused brother. "It'll hide our scent and make us harder to track."

For hours, they pushed on through the jungle, using every trick Ravi had gleaned from his years of TV watching. They created false trails, used plants to mask their scent, and moved in unpredictable patterns. Slowly, the sounds of pursuit faded, until finally, they found themselves alone in the vastness of the jungle.

As they paused to catch their breath, Ravi's brother turned to him with a mix of exhaustion and amazement. "Ravi," he panted, "how... How did you do all that? Where did you learn..."

Ravi couldn't help but laugh. "You'd be surprised what you can learn from TV if you pay attention," he said with a grin.

As they rested, Ravi filled his brother in on the events that had led him to this point. His brother listened with growing astonishment and Ravi was pleased to note respect. For the first time, Ravi felt like his brother was seeing him not as a lazy younger sibling, but as an equal – someone capable and resourceful.

But their ordeal was far from over. They were still deep in the jungle, miles from any civilization, and with angry kidnappers potentially still on their trail. As they discussed their next move, Ravi found himself drawing on knowledge from various survival shows, piecing together a plan to navigate back to safety.

"We need to find high ground," Ravi explained, recalling an episode of "Lost in the Wild." "From there, we might be able to spot a landmark or maybe even see signs of a town or village."

His brother nodded, a newfound trust evident in his eyes. As they set off again, Ravi felt a surge of confidence. He had already achieved what many, including himself, would have thought impossible. He had rescued his brother and outwitted dangerous criminals. Whatever challenges lay ahead, Ravi felt ready to face them.

As they trekked through the dense foliage, occasionally stopping to check their surroundings or listen for any signs of pursuit, Ravi's brother turned to him with a thoughtful expression. "You know, Ravi," he began, his voice tinged with a mix of admiration and regret, "I think we've all misjudged you. I'm sorry for the times I called you lazy or useless. What you've done... it's incredible."

Ravi felt a warmth spread through his chest at his brother's words. For years, he had lived in the shadow of his successful older sibling, always feeling inadequate in comparison. Now, here they were, equals in the face of adversity. "Thanks," Ravi replied softly. "But you know, I'm starting to think that maybe I misjudged myself too."

As they continued their journey, the brothers found themselves opening up to each other in a way they never had before. They shared stories, fears, and dreams, their bond growing stronger with each passing hour. Ravi realized that this harrowing adventure had given him something he had always longed for – a true connection with his brother.

The jungle, which had seemed so threatening before, now felt almost welcoming. Ravi found himself pointing out interesting plants and animals to his brother, sharing tidbits of information he had gleaned from countless nature documentaries. His brother listened with genuine interest, occasionally adding his own observations.

As the day wore on, they faced new challenges. A sudden tropical storm forced them to seek shelter, huddling together under a hastily constructed lean-to. Ravi's knowledge of jungle plants helped them find safe water sources and even some edible fruits to stave off hunger. With each obstacle overcome, Ravi felt his confidence grow. He was no longer just surviving by luck; he was thriving through knowledge and skill.

As night fell, they made camp in a small clearing. Sitting by a small fire, carefully shielded to avoid detection, the brothers talked late into the night. They discussed their childhood, their fears, and their hopes for the future. For the first time, Ravi felt truly seen and understood by his brother.

"You know, Ravi," his brother said as they prepared to sleep, "when we get back, things are going to be different. I won't let anyone underestimate you again – including me."

Ravi smiled in the darkness, feeling a sense of peace despite their precarious situation. Whatever happened next, he knew he had already gained something invaluable – self-respect and the respect of his brother.

As dawn broke, they set off again, determined to find their way back to civilization. The jungle seemed less daunting now, more like a challenging puzzle than an insurmountable obstacle. Ravi led the way, his senses alert, drawing on every bit of knowledge he had accumulated over years of vicarious adventures.

Little did they know that their greatest test was yet to come. As they pushed on towards what they hoped was safety, nature had one last, formidable challenge in store for them. But Ravi, once dismissed as a mere couch potato, was ready. He had discovered a strength within himself that no one, least of all himself, had known existed. Whatever lay ahead, he would face it – not alone, but side by side with his brother.

Chapter 6: Tracks in the Wild

As we transition from Ravi's initial challenges in the jungle, we now follow his journey as he begins to uncover crucial clues about his brother's kidnappers. In this chapter, Ravi's analytical skills, honed through years of television viewing, come to the forefront as he navigates the wild with growing confidence and determination.

The dense foliage of the jungle began to thin out as Ravi pushed forward, his eyes scanning the ground for any signs of human activity. The air was thick with humidity, and the cacophony of jungle sounds – bird calls, insect chirps, and the distant roar of what he hoped was just a waterfall – filled his ears. Despite the overwhelming sensory input, Ravi remained focused on his mission. He knew that every step could bring him closer to his brother, or to danger.

As he moved through a small clearing, something caught his eye. A flash of color that didn't belong in the natural palette of greens and browns. Crouching down, Ravi examined the object more closely. It was a small piece of bright red fabric, snagged on a thorny bush. His mind raced, recalling an episode of "CSI: Crime Scene Investigation" where the detectives had found a similar clue. "Trace evidence," he muttered to himself, carefully removing the fabric and placing it in his pocket.

The discovery energized Ravi, reinforcing his belief that he was on the right track. He began to move more deliberately, his eyes darting from the ground to the surrounding vegetation, searching for more out-of-place elements. It wasn't long before he spotted another anomaly – a series of footprints in a patch of muddy ground.

Ravi's heart raced as he knelt to examine the prints more closely. They were clearly human, and from the depth and spacing, he could tell they belonged to multiple people. "Just like in 'Criminal Minds,'" he thought, recalling how the FBI profilers would analyze crime scenes. He noticed that some of the prints were deeper than others, suggesting that one person might have been carrying a heavy load – or perhaps a captive.

As he followed the trail of footprints, Ravi's mind whirled with possibilities. He remembered a documentary about tracking he had once watched, where an expert tracker had explained how to determine the age of prints. Looking closely, he could see that the edges of these prints were still relatively sharp, with only minimal erosion from the jungle's constant moisture. They couldn't be more than a day old.

The trail led Ravi to a small stream, where the footprints disappeared. For a moment, he felt a pang of despair, thinking he had lost the trail. But then he recalled an episode of "Bear Grylls: Ultimate Survival" where the adventurer had tracked animals across a river. Ravi scanned the opposite bank, looking for any sign of disturbance. After a few tense minutes, he spotted it – a broken twig and a smear of mud on a rock, just where someone might have climbed out of the water.

Carefully crossing the stream, Ravi picked up the trail again on the other side. As he continued to follow the prints, he noticed other signs of human passage – a crushed fern here, a broken branch there. His confidence grew with each discovery. He was no longer just stumbling through the jungle; he was actively tracking his brother's kidnappers.

As the day wore on, Ravi's progress slowed. The jungle seemed to be getting denser, and the signs of human passage were becoming harder to spot. Just as he was considering stopping to rest, he caught a whiff of something out of place – smoke. His pulse quickened as he realized what this might mean.

Moving as quietly as he could, Ravi crept forward, using the thick vegetation for cover. The smell of smoke grew stronger, and soon he could hear faint voices carried on the breeze. Dropping to his stomach, he inched forward until he could peer through a gap in the foliage.

What he saw made his blood run cold. In a small clearing about fifty yards away, he could see a makeshift camp. Three rough-looking men sat around a small fire, talking in low voices. And there, tied to a tree at the edge of the clearing, was his brother.

Ravi's first instinct was to rush forward, to attempt a rescue then and there. But he forced himself to remain still, remembering countless scenes from action movies where the hero's impulsive actions had led to disaster. Instead, he observed, taking in every detail of the camp and its occupants.

He noted the weapons the men carried – two had rifles slung over their shoulders, while the third had a pistol tucked into his waistband. He watched their movements, trying to gauge their level of alertness and their routines. Most importantly, he studied his brother, looking for any signs of injury or ill-treatment.

As he lay there, barely daring to breathe, Ravi's mind raced. He knew he couldn't take on three armed men by himself. He needed a plan, and he needed more information. Drawing on everything he had learned from years of watching spy thrillers and police procedurals, he began to formulate a strategy.

First, he needed to find a way to communicate with his brother without alerting the kidnappers. Then, he would need to create a diversion to separate the men. Finally, he would need to neutralize their weapons somehow. It was a daunting task, but as he watched the camp, Ravi felt a surge of determination. He had come this far, defying everyone's expectations. He wasn't about to give up now.

As the sun began to set, casting long shadows through the jungle, Ravi carefully retreated from his observation point. He needed to find a safe place to rest and plan his next move. As he made his way back through the dense foliage, he reflected on how far he had come. Just days ago, he had been nothing more than a couch potato in the eyes of his family. Now, he was on the verge of attempting a daring rescue.

The irony wasn't lost on Ravi. All those hours spent watching television, which his family had seen as a waste of time, had given him the knowledge and skills he needed to track down his brother. He allowed himself a small smile at the thought. If – no, when – he succeeded in this rescue, he would have quite a story to tell.

As night fell, Ravi found a small, sheltered spot to make camp. As he lay there, listening to the night sounds of the jungle, his mind was already racing ahead to the next day. He knew the challenges that lay ahead would be the greatest he had faced yet. But he also knew that with each step, each discovery, he was getting closer to his goal.

The tension was building, the danger was growing, but so was Ravi's determination. As he drifted off to sleep, his last thoughts were of his brother, and the promise he had made to bring him home. Tomorrow would be a crucial day, and Ravi was ready to face whatever challenges it might bring.

As we move into the next chapter, Ravi will face his most harrowing experience yet. His newfound skills will be put to the ultimate test as he comes face to face with the kidnappers, risking everything in a desperate attempt to avoid detection and keep his rescue mission alive.

Chapter 7: A Close Call

As we left Ravi navigating the treacherous jungle terrain in the previous chapter, we now find him facing an even more perilous situation. The search for his kidnapped brother has led him deeper into the heart of the wilderness, and with each step, the stakes grow higher.

Ravi's heart pounded in his chest as he crouched behind a large, moss-covered boulder. The sounds of the jungle seemed to amplify around him – the chirping of insects, the distant call of exotic birds, and the rustling of leaves in the gentle breeze. But it was another sound that had sent him diving for cover: voices. Human voices, rough and unfamiliar, speaking in hushed tones just beyond his hiding place.

For a moment, Ravi closed his eyes, willing his breathing to slow and his mind to focus. He had come so far, pushed himself beyond limits he never knew he had, all in the name of rescuing his brother. Now, he found himself mere meters away from the very people who had torn his family apart. The kidnappers were so close he could almost reach out and touch them.

As he steadied himself, Ravi's mind flickered back to a late-night TV marathon of spy thrillers he had once watched. In one particular scene, the protagonist had used an improvised periscope to observe his enemies without exposing himself. With careful, deliberate movements, Ravi reached into his backpack and pulled out a small compact mirror he had brought along for signaling purposes. He also extracted a long, straight stick he had picked up earlier in his journey.

Using the shoelace from one of his boots, Ravi carefully tied the mirror to one end of the stick at an angle. Slowly, he raised his makeshift periscope above the boulder, adjusting it until he could see the reflection of the area beyond his hiding spot.

What he saw made his blood run cold. Three men, heavily armed and dressed in camouflage, were hunched over a crude map spread out on a fallen log. Their fingers traced paths through the dense foliage, and though Ravi couldn't make out their words, their intent was clear. They were planning their next move, and Ravi had a sinking feeling that it involved relocating his brother.

As he watched, one of the men suddenly looked up, his eyes scanning the surrounding area. Ravi's heart leapt into his throat, and he quickly lowered his periscope, pressing his back against the cool surface of the boulder. Has he been spotted? The seconds ticked by like hours as he waited, barely daring to breathe.

After what felt like an eternity, the voices resumed their hushed conversation. Ravi let out a silent sigh of relief, but he knew he wasn't out of danger yet. He needed to move, to find a safer vantage point where he could gather more information without risking detection.

Recalling a nature documentary about jungle camouflage, Ravi began to formulate a plan. He remembered how certain animals used their surroundings to blend in, becoming virtually invisible to predators and prey alike. With slow, deliberate movements, he began to gather leaves, mud, and small branches from the forest floor around him.

Carefully, Ravi smeared mud across his face and exposed skin, grimacing at the earthy smell and cool, slimy texture. He then began to weave leaves and small branches into his clothes, creating a pattern that mimicked the dappled sunlight filtering through the canopy above. As he worked, he couldn't help but smile wryly at the thought of what his family would say if they could see him now – Ravi, the couch potato, covered in mud and leaves in the middle of the jungle.

Once he was satisfied with his camouflage, Ravi took a deep breath and prepared to move. He knew that stealth was crucial; one snapped twig or rustled leaf could give him away. Slowly, painfully slowly, he began to inch away from the boulder, keeping his body low to the ground.

Every movement was calculated, every pause timed with the natural sounds of the forest. Ravi found himself drawing on every nature show he had ever watched, every wildlife documentary that had kept him glued to the screen late into the night. He moved like a stalking predator, his eyes constantly scanning for potential hiding spots and escape routes.

As he crept through the underbrush, Ravi's mind raced. He was closer to finding his brother than ever before, but he was also in more danger than he had been since starting this journey. The reality of his situation hit him like a physical blow – he was alone, untrained, and up against armed and dangerous men. For a moment, fear threatened to overwhelm him.

But then, unbidden, a memory surfaced. It was of his brother, years ago, teaching a young Ravi how to ride a bicycle. "Don't look at what might make you fall," his brother had said. "Look at where you want to go." Ravi clung to that memory, to the sound of his brother's encouraging voice. He couldn't afford to focus on his fear or his inadequacies. He had to keep his eyes on the goal – finding and rescuing his brother.

With renewed determination, Ravi continued his careful progress through the jungle. He moved from tree to tree, using the thick trunks as cover. His camouflage proved effective; twice, he froze in place as one of the kidnappers passed nearby, oblivious to his presence.

As the day wore on, Ravi shadowed the group, always keeping a safe distance but never letting them out of his sight. He watched as they broke camp and began to move, confirming his fears that they were relocating. Every fiber of his being screamed to rush in, to confront them and demand his brother's release. But the rational part of his mind, the part that had absorbed countless strategic and tactical scenarios from his TV shows, knew that such an action would be suicidal.

Instead, Ravi focused on gathering information. He noted the direction they were traveling, the supplies they carried, and most importantly, any mentions of his brother. Though he couldn't make out most of their conversation, he caught snippets here and there – enough to know that his brother was alive and being held at a new location.

As the sun began to set, casting long shadows through the jungle, Ravi found himself facing a difficult decision. The kidnappers had made camp for the night, setting up a small, well-concealed site that would be easy to defend. Ravi knew he needed rest too, but the thought of losing track of the group filled him with anxiety.

In the end, exhaustion made the decision for him. Ravi found a secluded spot within earshot of the kidnappers' camp, wedging himself between the gnarled roots of a massive tree. As he settled in for the night, he couldn't help but reflect on how far he had come.

Just days ago, he had been nothing more than a couch potato, content to experience the world through his television screen. Now, he was living an adventure more intense and dangerous than any he had ever watched. The irony wasn't lost on him – all those hours of TV viewing, which his family had dismissed as wasteful, had given him the knowledge he needed to survive in this hostile environment and stay one step ahead of the kidnappers.

As Ravi drifted off into an uneasy sleep, his last thoughts were of his brother. "I'm coming," he whispered into the darkness. "Just hold on a little longer."

The night passed fitfully, with Ravi jolting awake at every unfamiliar sound. As the first light of dawn began to filter through the canopy, he was already alert and ready to move. He knew the kidnappers would be breaking camp soon, and he couldn't afford to lose them.

Quickly checking his camouflage and gathering his meager supplies, Ravi prepared for another day of careful stalking. As he moved into position, he couldn't shake the feeling that today would be different. Something was going to change – he could feel it in his bones.

Little did Ravi know that his journey was about to take an unexpected turn. As he continued to trail the kidnappers, fate was preparing to introduce a new element into his rescue mission – an element that would test his resourcefulness and courage in ways he had never imagined. But that, as they say, is a story for another chapter.

Chapter 8: The Unexpected Ally

As Ravi ventured deeper into the dense jungle, the weight of his mission grew heavier with each step. The search for his kidnapped brother had led him far from the comfort of his couch and television, yet the knowledge gained from countless hours of watching survival shows was proving invaluable. The verdant canopy above filtered the sunlight, casting dappled shadows on the forest floor, and the air hung thick with humidity and the cacophony of unseen creatures. It was in this alien environment that Ravi's path would intersect with an unexpected ally, setting the stage for a series of events that would challenge his preconceptions and push his TV-acquired skills to their limits.

The encounter came without warning. As Ravi carefully picked his way through a particularly overgrown section of the jungle, he suddenly found himself face-to-face with a weathered local man. The man's appearance was a stark contrast to Ravi's city-dweller attire – he wore simple, worn clothing that seemed to blend seamlessly with the surrounding foliage. His deeply lined face spoke of years spent under the harsh jungle sun, and his eyes held a mix of wariness and curiosity as they studied Ravi.

For a moment, both stood frozen, sizing each other up. Ravi's mind raced, recalling episodes of travel shows where intrepid hosts made first contact with indigenous tribes. He raised his hand in what he hoped was a universal gesture of peace, half-expecting the man to reciprocate with some form of ritualistic greeting he'd seen on National Geographic.

"Namaste," Ravi ventured, his voice cracking slightly from disuse and nervousness. To his surprise and mild disappointment, the man simply chuckled and responded in accented but clear Hindi.

"You're a long way from home, city boy," the man said, his tone a mixture of amusement and concern. "What brings you to this unforgiving place?"

Ravi's relief at finding someone who spoke a language he understood was palpable. He quickly explained his mission to rescue his kidnapped brother, the words tumbling out in a rush of pent-up emotion and desperation. The man listened intently, his expression growing more serious with each detail Ravi shared.

As Ravi finished his tale, the man introduced himself as Kiran, a former guide who now lived a solitary life in the jungle. "Your brother's situation is grave," Kiran said, his voice low and tinged with worry. "The men you seek are known to me. They are dangerous, without mercy. But perhaps, with my knowledge of the land and your... unique skills, we may yet save him."

Ravi felt a surge of hope at Kiran's words, but it was tempered by a nagging doubt. How could his "unique skills" – gleaned entirely from television – possibly measure up in this life-or-death situation? As if reading his thoughts, Kiran smiled wryly.

"Do not underestimate the power of knowledge, regardless of its source," he said. "Come, let us make camp. We have much to discuss, and you have much to learn about the reality of jungle survival."

As they set about gathering materials for a shelter, Ravi's TV-inspired instincts kicked in. He began to explain the importance of finding dry wood for fire and the best leaves for thatching, quoting verbatim from an episode of "Survivorman." Kiran listened with a mix of amusement and genuine interest, occasionally correcting Ravi's misconceptions or adding local knowledge that no TV show could provide.

Their shelter half-built, Ravi's stomach growled audibly. Kiran laughed, a warm, rich sound that seemed to lighten the oppressive jungle atmosphere. "Ah, city boy, let me show you how we find food here. It's a bit different from ordering takeout, I'm afraid."

What followed was a crash course in jungle foraging that both validated and challenged Ravi's TV-acquired knowledge. He correctly identified several edible plants, much to Kiran's surprise, but also nearly poisoned himself by mistaking a toxic berry for one he'd seen Bear Grylls eat on "Man vs. Wild."

"Remember, Ravi," Kiran admonished gently as he knocked the berries from Ravi's hand, "what works in one part of the world may kill you in another. Nature demands respect and careful observation, not blind imitation."

As night fell and they sat around a small, carefully managed fire, Kiran shared vital information about Ravi's brother's likely location. He spoke of a hidden valley, deep in the heart of the jungle, where the kidnappers were known to operate. The journey would be treacherous, filled with natural obstacles and the constant threat of discovery.

Ravi listened intently, his mind racing with both excitement and fear. This was it – the real-life adventure he had always dreamed of, yet never truly believed he'd experience. But as Kiran described the dangers ahead, doubts began to creep in. Could he really do this? Was he putting too much faith in knowledge gained from a screen?

Sensing Ravi's inner turmoil, Kiran placed a reassuring hand on his shoulder. "Your brother's life hangs in the balance, but do not let fear paralyze you. The journey ahead will test you in ways you cannot imagine, but remember this: the strength to overcome lies not in your muscles or even in your mind, but in your heart. Your love for your brother, your determination to save him – these are powers that no TV show can teach, but which will carry you through the darkest moments."

Ravi nodded, feeling a renewed sense of purpose. As they settled in for the night, the jungle's nocturnal symphony rising around them, he reflected on the strange twist of fate that had brought him here. He had always been the family's "couch potato," dismissed as lazy and unambitious. Yet here he was, deep in the wilderness, about to embark on a rescue mission that would challenge every fiber of his being.

The irony wasn't lost on him – all those hours of watching TV, once seen as a waste, had given him a foundation of knowledge that might just save his brother's life. But Kiran's presence and wisdom had shown him that real-world experience was irreplaceable. As he drifted off to sleep, Ravi realized that his true journey of growth and self-discovery was only just beginning.

Dawn broke over the jungle, painting the sky in hues of pink and gold that filtered through the dense canopy. Ravi awoke to find Kiran already up and preparing a simple breakfast of fruits and roots. As they ate, Kiran outlined their plan for the day – a grueling trek through some of the most challenging terrains the jungle had to offer.

"We must move swiftly and silently," Kiran explained, his voice low and serious. "The kidnappers have eyes and ears everywhere. One misstep, one careless sound, and all could be lost."

Ravi nodded, trying to quell the nervous energy that threatened to overwhelm him. As, they set out, he found himself constantly comparing the real jungle to the sanitized version he'd seen on TV. The humidity was oppressive, clinging to his skin and making every movement a struggle. The ground beneath his feet was treacherous, a mix of slippery leaves, hidden roots, and unstable soil that demanded constant vigilance.

Yet, as the day wore on, Ravi began to find a rhythm. His TV-inspired knowledge, while often requiring adjustment, proved surprisingly useful. He correctly identified several plants that could be used for hydration, impressing Kiran with his recall of a documentary on jungle botany. When they encountered a fast-flowing river, Ravi suggested a method of crossing he'd seen on an adventure show, which Kiran agreed was sound after some modification.

Their progress, however, was not without its share of humorous mishaps. At one point, Ravi attempted to swing across a small ravine using a vine, just as he'd seen countless explorers do on screen. The result was less Tarzan and more slapstick comedy, with Ravi ending up face-first in a mud puddle, much to Kiran's barely concealed amusement.

"Perhaps we should stick to walking for now," Kiran suggested, helping a sheepish Ravi to his feet. "The jungle is not a movie set, my friend. It does not always cooperate with our dramatic intentions."

As they pushed deeper into the wilderness, Kiran shared stories of the land and its people. He spoke of ancient tribal conflicts, of the delicate balance between man and nature, and of the encroachment of the modern world on this primeval realm. Ravi listened, fascinated, realizing how much depth and complexity lay behind the simplified narratives often presented on television.

Their conversation was suddenly interrupted by the distant sound of voices. Kiran held up a hand, signaling for silence, his entire demeanor changing in an instant. Gone was the affable guide; in his place stood a man of the jungle, alert and dangerous as any predator.

"The kidnappers," he whispered, barely audible above the ambient sounds of the forest. "They're closer than I expected. We must be very careful now."

Ravi's heart pounded in his chest as they crouched low, inching forward with agonizing slowness. Through a gap in the foliage, he caught a glimpse of rough-looking men, heavily armed, moving through a clearing ahead. Among them, looking haggard but alive, was a familiar figure – Ravi's brother.

The sight sent a jolt of emotion through Ravi – relief that his brother was alive, fear for his condition, and a burning desire to rush to his aid. But Kiran's firm grip on his arm held him back.

"Patience," Kiran breathed. "We are outmanned and outgunned. We must be smart, not brave. Remember your TV heroes – did they not always have a clever plan?"

Ravi nodded, forcing himself to think rationally. As they watched the group move off into the distance, he began to formulate a strategy, drawing on every relevant scene he could remember from his vast mental library of television.

As night fell once more, Ravi and Kiran made camp well hidden from any potential patrols. Over a cold meal – they dared not risk a fire – they discussed their options. Ravi's plan, a patchwork of ideas culled from various shows, was ambitious and risky. Kiran listened with a mix of skepticism and grudging admiration.

"It's crazy," he said finally. "But in this situation, going crazy might be our only option. We'll need to refine it, adapt it to the realities of our situation. But the core idea... it just might work."

As they settled in for a restless night, the gravity of their situation weighed heavily on Ravi. Tomorrow would bring the greatest challenge of his life – a real-world test of everything he'd absorbed through years of vicarious adventures. As he drifted off to sleep, his last conscious thought was a silent promise to his brother: "Hold on. We're coming for you."

The jungle seemed to hold its breath, as if aware of the drama about to unfold within its shadowy depths. In the darkness, Ravi's mind raced with possibilities and fears, his TV-inspired plan seeming simultaneously brilliant and foolish. But with Kiran's guidance and his own unexpected reserves of courage, he knew that tomorrow would be the day that would define not just this adventure, but his entire life. The couch potato had become a jungle warrior, and the next chapter of his incredible journey was about to begin.

Chapter 9: Nature's Fury

As Ravi pushed deeper into the jungle, the air grew thick with moisture, and the canopy above seemed to close in around him. The events of the past few days had tested him in ways he never imagined, but nothing could have prepared him for the challenge that lay ahead. Nature, it seemed, had one more trial in store for the unlikely hero.

The first drops of rain fell softly, barely noticeable through the dense foliage. Ravi paused, tilting his head back to observe the darkening sky through gaps in the leaves. A memory flickered in his mind – a documentary he had watched on extreme weather phenomena. The narrator's voice echoed in his thoughts, "In tropical regions, seemingly harmless rainstorms can quickly escalate into dangerous flash floods."

As if on cue, the gentle patter of raindrops transformed into a deafening roar. Water cascaded from the sky in sheets, turning the forest floor into a treacherous quagmire. Ravi's heart raced as he realized the gravity of his situation. The path he had been following was rapidly disappearing beneath a torrent of muddy water.

Panic threatened to overwhelm him, but Ravi forced himself to take a deep breath. He closed his eyes, searching his memory for any information that could help him navigate this perilous situation. Another fragment of the documentary surfaced – advice on finding high ground during flash floods.

With renewed determination, Ravi scanned his surroundings. Through the curtain of rain, he spotted a rocky outcropping a short distance away. It wasn't much, but it was higher than the rapidly rising water level. He knew he had to act fast.

Ravi began to move, each step a battle against the surging water and slippery mud. The weight of his backpack threatened to throw him off balance, but he pressed on, driven by the urgency of his situation and the memory of his brother's face. As he struggled forward, Ravi couldn't help but marvel at the irony of his predicament. Here he was, fighting for survival in the heart of the jungle, armed with nothing but knowledge gleaned from countless hours of television.

The water was now knee-deep, its current strong enough to sweep him off his feet if he wasn't careful. Ravi's muscles screamed in protest as he fought against the flow, inching closer to the rocky sanctuary. A fallen tree, caught in the flood, hurtled towards him. With a surge of adrenaline, Ravi lunged forward, narrowly avoiding a collision that could have spelled disaster.

Finally, after what felt like an eternity, Ravi reached the base of the rocky outcropping. His hands, numb from the cold rain, scrambled for purchase on the slick surface. Slowly, painfully, he pulled himself up, collapsing onto a relatively flat area just as another surge of water rushed beneath him.

As Ravi lay there, gasping for breath, the full weight of what he had just accomplished hit him. He had faced nature's fury and emerged victorious. A quiet laugh bubbled up from his chest, a mixture of relief and disbelief. If only his family could see him now – Ravi, the couch potato, outsmarting a flash flood in the middle of the jungle.

The rain continued to pour, but from his elevated position, Ravi felt a sense of security. He took the opportunity to assess his situation and plan his next move. The documentary had mentioned that tropical storms, while intense, often passed quickly. All he needed to do was wait it out.

As he sat there, watching the chaos of the flood below, Ravi reflected on how far he had come. Just a week ago, his greatest challenge had been deciding which TV show to watch next. Now, he was drawing on that very knowledge to survive in one of the most unforgiving environments on Earth.

The irony wasn't lost on him. For years, his family had berated him for his television habits, calling it a waste of time. Yet here he was, alive and pushing forward, thanks in large part to the information he had absorbed from those countless hours in front of the screen. It was a vindication of sorts, though Ravi knew the real test was still to come.

As the hours passed and the rain began to subside, Ravi found himself pondering the nature of strength and resilience. He had always thought of these qualities in terms of physical prowess – something his athletic older brother had in spades. But now, faced with the challenges of the jungle, Ravi was discovering a different kind of strength within himself. It was a strength born of adaptability, quick thinking, and the ability to recall and apply knowledge in critical situations.

The realization filled him with a newfound confidence. He might not have his brother's muscles or his parents' academic achievements, but he had something uniquely his own – a vast repository of knowledge and the creativity to use it in unexpected ways. This jungle adventure was proving to be more than just a rescue mission; it was a journey of self-discovery.

As the flood waters began to recede, Ravi carefully made his way back down to solid ground. The jungle around him bore the scars of the violent storm – fallen branches, uprooted plants, and debris scattered everywhere. But amidst the destruction, Ravi noticed signs of life persevering. A colorful bird emerged from its shelter, shaking water from its feathers. Insects began their chorus anew. The jungle, like Ravi himself, was resilient.

With renewed determination, Ravi set off once more on his quest to find his brother. The storm had been a setback, yes, but it had also been a valuable lesson. Nature was unpredictable and often harsh, but with knowledge and quick thinking, even the most daunting obstacles could be overcome.

As he navigated the altered landscape, Ravi found himself recalling other snippets of information from various nature documentaries. He identified edible plants, avoiding those that could be poisonous. He listened for the sounds of running water, knowing it could lead him to a stream – a potential source of fresh water and perhaps even a clue to his brother's whereabouts.

The sun began to peek through the dissipating clouds, casting dappled shadows on the forest floor. Ravi paused for a moment, closing his eyes and feeling the warmth on his face. It was a simple pleasure, but after the ordeal he had just been through, it felt like a luxury. He allowed himself a small smile, remembering how he used to complain about the glare on the TV screen when sunlight streamed through the living room windows. Now, that same sunlight felt like a blessing, a sign that he was still alive and moving forward.

As Ravi continued his journey, he found that the storm had left behind more than just destruction. In some areas, the flood had carved new paths through the undergrowth, creating shortcuts he could use to make up for lost time. In others, it had exposed hidden features of the landscape – rock formations, animal tracks, and even man-made markings that might have otherwise gone unnoticed.

One such discovery caught Ravi's eye – a series of notches carved into a tree trunk, partially revealed by the erosion of soil around its base. His mind immediately went to an episode of a survival show he had watched, where the host had explained various tracking techniques used by indigenous tribes. Could these marks be a trail sign left by the kidnappers? Or perhaps by his brother in an attempt to leave a clue?

Excitement coursed through Ravi's veins as he examined the markings more closely. They were deliberate, that much was clear, and they seemed to point in a specific direction. It wasn't much to go on, but in this vast, unforgiving jungle, any lead was worth pursuing.

As Ravi prepared to follow this new trail, he couldn't help but marvel at how his perspective had shifted. The jungle, which had initially seemed like an impenetrable, hostile environment, was now revealing its secrets to him. Every plant, every sound, every change in the terrain held potential information. He was learning to read the landscape, much like he used to read the intricate plotlines of his favorite TV shows.

The parallels between his current situation and the countless adventures he had witnessed on screen were not lost on Ravi. How many times had he watched protagonists face seemingly insurmountable odds, only to emerge victorious through wit, perseverance, and a bit of luck? He had always admired those characters, living vicariously through their exploits. Now, he was writing his own adventure story, with himself as the unlikely hero.

As the day wore on, Ravi found himself pushing his body to its limits. The physical toll of his journey was beginning to catch up with him, but he refused to give in to fatigue. Every step brought him closer to his brother, closer to proving to himself and his family that he was more than just a lazy couch potato.

The jungle seemed to sense his determination, throwing new challenges his way at every turn. A steep ravine forced him to improvise a makeshift bridge using fallen logs. A surprise encounter with a venomous snake tested his newly acquired knowledge of jungle wildlife. Each obstacle overcome added to Ravi's growing confidence and resourcefulness.

As the sun began to set, painting the sky in brilliant hues of orange and pink, Ravi found a suitable spot to make camp for the night. He went through the motions of setting up shelter and starting a small fire, tasks that would have seemed impossible to him just a week ago. Now, they were almost second nature.

Sitting by the flickering flames, Ravi allowed himself a moment of reflection. He thought about his family back home, probably sick with worry. He thought about his brother, hoping against hope that he was safe and that Ravi would reach him in time. And he thought about himself – the person he had been before this adventure, and the person he was becoming.

The jungle night closed in around him, alive with the sounds of nocturnal creatures. As Ravi prepared to get some much-needed rest, he couldn't shake the feeling that tomorrow would bring him closer to his goal. The storm had been a formidable opponent, but he had emerged stronger, more capable, and more determined than ever.

As he drifted off to sleep, Ravi's mind wandered to the next chapter of his journey. The kidnappers' lair couldn't be far now. He would need all his wit, all his newly acquired skills, and perhaps a bit of that TV-inspired luck to face the challenges ahead. But for the first time since embarking on this perilous quest, Ravi felt truly ready for whatever the jungle – and the kidnappers – might throw at him.

With the sound of the jungle's night symphony in his ears and the warmth of the fire on his face, Ravi fell into a deep, restful sleep. Tomorrow would bring new trials, but also new opportunities. And Ravi, the once-ridiculed couch potato turned jungle survivor, was ready to face them head-on.

Chapter 10: The Kidnappers' Lair

As Ravi ventured deeper into the heart of the jungle, the air grew thick with anticipation. The information he had gleaned from his unexpected ally proved invaluable, guiding him towards what he hoped would be his brother's location. The dense foliage thinned slightly, revealing glimpses of a clearing ahead. Ravi's heart raced as he realized he might be on the verge of discovering the kidnappers' hideout.

Recalling an episode of his favorite crime drama, Ravi knew the importance of gathering intelligence before making any bold moves. He crouched low, inching forward with painstaking care to avoid snapping any twigs or rustling leaves. The jungle seemed to hold its breath with him, the usual cacophony of wildlife momentarily subdued as if nature itself was conspiring to aid his stealth.

As he neared the edge of the clearing, Ravi's eyes widened at the sight before him. A ramshackle structure stood in the center, cobbled together from corrugated metal sheets and weathered wooden planks. It was clear that this was no ordinary jungle dwelling; the makeshift fortifications and the nervous pacing of armed men around the perimeter spoke volumes about its true purpose.

Ravi's mind raced, recalling countless episodes of spy thrillers and police procedurals. He knew he needed to observe, to understand the patterns and routines of the kidnappers if he had any hope of rescuing his brother. Finding a concealed spot with a good vantage point, Ravi settled in for a long watch, his body tense but his mind sharp and focused.

Hours passed like minutes as Ravi meticulously noted every detail. He counted the guards, memorized their patrol routes, and studied the structure of the hideout. His keen eye, honed by years of scrutinizing crime scene investigations on TV, picked up on subtle details that might prove crucial: a loose board in the wall, a guard who seemed less attentive than the others, the timing of shift changes.

As the sun began to dip below the horizon, casting long shadows across the clearing, Ravi's patience was rewarded. A commotion near the entrance of the hideout caught his attention. His breath caught in his throat as he saw a figure being roughly shoved outside – it was his brother, looking haggard but alive. The sight filled Ravi with a mixture of relief and renewed determination. He watched intently as his brother was allowed a brief moment outside, presumably for some fresh air, before being hustled back into the structure.

This glimpse of his brother ignited a fire in Ravi's chest. He was close, so tantalizingly close to his goal. But he knew that rushing in blindly would be foolish. He needed a plan, a strategy that would maximize his chances of success while minimizing the risk to his brother's life.

Drawing on his vast repository of TV-inspired knowledge, Ravi began to formulate a rescue strategy. He recalled an episode of a military drama where a small team had infiltrated a heavily guarded compound. The key, he remembered, was not brute force but misdirection and clever use of the environment.

Ravi's eyes scanned the surroundings, taking in every tree, every rock, every shadow that could potentially be used to his advantage. He noted the position of the sun, remembering a survival show that emphasized the importance of using natural light and darkness strategically.

As night fell, Ravi's planning intensified. He sketched crude maps in the dirt, plotting approach routes and escape paths. He inventoried his meager supplies, his mind racing with possibilities on how each item could be repurposed for his mission. A shoelace could become a tripwire, a water bottle could serve as a distraction device, his brightly colored t-shirt could be used to create a decoy.

Ravi's thoughts turned to the guards. He had observed their behaviors, their habits, their weaknesses. One guard had a penchant for dozing off during the late-night shift. Another had a habit of wandering away from his post for smoke breaks. These human flaws, so often exploited in the TV shows Ravi loved, now presented real-world opportunities.

As he planned, Ravi couldn't help but marvel at how his years of TV watching, once dismissed as wasteful by his family, were now proving to be his greatest asset. Each show, each episode, each dramatic scene had deposited nuggets of knowledge in his mind, creating a vast database of strategies and techniques that he was now drawing upon in this most critical of moments.

The irony wasn't lost on Ravi. Here he was, the family's supposed "couch potato," orchestrating a rescue mission that would make any action hero proud. He allowed himself a small smile, imagining the look on his family's faces when – not if, but when – he returned with his brother in tow.

But Ravi knew that planning was only half the battle. The true test would come in the execution. He thought back to all the times he had shouted advice at the TV screen, critiquing the decisions of fictional heroes. Now, he was the one who would have to make those split-second choices, with real lives hanging in the balance.

The weight of the responsibility settled heavily on Ravi's shoulders. This wasn't a TV show where the hero always triumphs against impossible odds. This was real life, with real dangers and real consequences. For a moment, doubt crept into Ravi's mind. Was he truly capable of pulling this off? Was he foolish to think that his

TV-derived knowledge could stand up to the harsh realities of this situation?

But then Ravi thought of his brother, trapped and alone, counting on him. He thought of his family back home, worried sick and probably imagining the worst. He couldn't let them down. He had come too far, overcome too many obstacles to falter now.

With renewed determination, Ravi refocused on his planning. He began to piece together a multi-stage strategy, drawing inspiration from various sources. The initial distraction would be inspired by a heist movie, creating chaos to thin out the guard presence. The infiltration would mirror a spy thriller, using stealth and misdirection to penetrate the hideout's defenses. And the actual rescue would channel the teamwork and precise timing he had seen in countless action films.

As Ravi fine-tuned his plan, he realized that his greatest strength lay not in physical prowess or specialized training, but in his ability to think creatively and adapt quickly. His mind, shaped by years of absorbing diverse scenarios and solutions from TV, was his most potent weapon.

The night deepened, and Ravi knew that the time for action was drawing near. He had observed that the guards were at their least alert in the early hours of the morning, just before dawn. This would be his window of opportunity, the critical moment when all his planning and preparation would be put to the test.

Ravi began his final preparations, his movements deliberate and focused. He gathered materials for his distractions, prepared his makeshift tools, and ran through his plan one last time in his head. Each step, each contingency was clear in his mind, a testament to the hours of meticulous planning.

As he worked, Ravi reflected on the journey that had brought him to this point. From the comfort of his living room couch to the heart of a dangerous jungle, he had transformed in ways he never thought possible. The lazy, unfocused boy his family knew had been replaced by a determined, resourceful young man ready to face whatever challenges lay ahead.

With his preparations complete, Ravi settled in to wait for the perfect moment to strike. The jungle around him was quiet, as if holding its breath in anticipation of the drama about to unfold. In these final moments of calm before the storm, Ravi's thoughts turned to his brother. He imagined the reunion, the relief, the joy of bringing him home safely. This vision steeled his resolve, banishing any lingering doubts or fears.

As the first hints of dawn began to lighten the eastern sky, Ravi took a deep breath. It was time. With a silent prayer and a heart full of determination, he prepared to put his plan into action. The couch potato was about to become a real-life hero, and the kidnappers' lair was about to face a challenge it never saw coming.

Moving with purpose, Ravi began to implement the first phase of his plan. He carefully placed his homemade distractions around the perimeter of the clearing, each one designed to create confusion and draw the guards away from their posts. With trembling hands but unwavering resolve, he set the timer on his makeshift devices, knowing that once activated, there would be no turning back.

As he worked, Ravi's mind raced through countless scenarios, anticipating potential obstacles and formulating contingencies. He knew that no plan, no matter how well-conceived, survived first contact with the enemy unchanged. Flexibility would be key, and Ravi was prepared to improvise as needed, drawing on his vast mental library of TV-inspired solutions.

With the last of his preparations in place, Ravi retreated to his designated starting position. His heart pounded in his chest, a mix of fear and exhilaration coursing through his veins. In just a few short minutes, the relative calm of the jungle would be shattered, and Ravi would be thrust into the most challenging and dangerous situation of his life.

As he waited for his devices to activate, Ravi allowed himself one final moment of reflection. He thought of his journey, of the doubts and hardships he had overcome to reach this point. He thought of his family, of their low expectations and his own unfulfilled potential. And he thought of his brother, whose life now hung in the balance, dependent on the success of this audacious rescue attempt.

The first rays of sunlight began to pierce through the canopy, casting dappled shadows across the forest floor. Ravi took a deep breath, centering himself for the challenge ahead. In that moment, he felt a strange sense of calm wash over him. Whatever the outcome, he knew that he had already proven himself in ways he never thought possible.

Suddenly, the stillness of the morning was shattered by a series of loud bangs and flashes. Ravi's distractions had activated, throwing the kidnappers' camp into chaos. Shouts of alarm and confusion filled the air as guards scrambled to investigate the disturbances.

This was it. The moment of truth had arrived. With a silent prayer and a heart full of determination, Ravi sprang into action. The rescue mission had begun, and the next chapter of his incredible journey was about to unfold.

As Ravi moved swiftly towards the kidnappers' lair, he couldn't help but feel a sense of anticipation for what lay ahead. The challenges he had faced so far had tested him in ways he never imagined, but he knew that the true test was yet to come. With his brother's life at stake and the eyes of his family metaphorically upon him, Ravi steeled himself for the confrontation that awaited. The journey from couch potato to hero was nearing its climax, and Ravi was determined to see it through to the end, no matter what obstacles he might encounter.

73

Chapter 11: Rescue Gone Wrong

As Ravi crouched behind a large boulder, his heart pounding in his chest, he realized that his carefully crafted plan had just fallen apart. The rescue attempt he had meticulously prepared for over the past few days had gone terribly wrong. He could hear the angry shouts of the kidnappers echoing through the dense forest, growing louder with each passing moment. The bitter taste of failure filled his mouth as he tried to catch his breath and gather his thoughts.

Just minutes ago, Ravi had been filled with confidence. He had spent days observing the kidnappers' hideout, noting their routines and weaknesses. His strategy had been inspired by countless episodes of crime dramas and spy thrillers he had binge-watched back home. He had even practiced his moves, imagining himself as the hero who would swoop in and save the day. But reality, as he was now learning the hard way, was far more unpredictable and dangerous than any scripted television show.

The plan had seemed foolproof in his mind. Ravi had waited for the moment when most of the kidnappers left the hideout, leaving only two guards behind. He had created a distraction using some firecrackers he had brought along, hoping the noise would draw the guards away from their post. Then, he would sneak in, free his brother, and they would both escape into the jungle before anyone realized what had happened.

At first, everything had gone according to plan. The firecrackers had worked perfectly, creating a cacophony of noise that had the desired effect. The guards, startled and confused, had moved away from their posts to investigate. Ravi had seized the opportunity, his heart racing with excitement as he slipped into the hideout. He had found his brother, tied up but unharmed, in a small, dank room. The look of shock and relief on his brother's face when he saw Ravi had been indescribable.

But that's where things had started to unravel. As Ravi fumbled with the ropes binding his brother, his trembling hands betraying his nervousness, they had heard voices approaching. The guards had returned much faster than Ravi had anticipated. In a moment of panic, Ravi had made a critical error. Instead of hiding or trying to bluff his way out, he had bolted, leaving his brother behind.

Now, as he hid behind the boulder, the gravity of his mistake hit him like a ton of bricks. He had not only failed to rescue his brother but had also alerted the kidnappers to his presence. The element of surprise, his most significant advantage, was now gone. Worse still, he had abandoned his brother in a moment of cowardice. The shame of it burned in his chest, threatening to overwhelm him.

As the kidnappers' voices grew closer, Ravi's mind raced, desperately trying to find a way out of this mess. He thought back to all the TV shows he had watched, searching for any nugget of wisdom that could help him now. Suddenly, a scene from a heist movie flashed in his mind. In the film, the protagonist had used misdirection to escape a similar situation. Could that work here?

With trembling hands, Ravi reached into his backpack and pulled out his remaining firecrackers. He only had a few left, but they might be enough. Taking a deep breath to steady himself, he lit the fuse and threw the firecrackers as far as he could in the opposite direction from where he was hiding.

The explosion of noise that followed was deafening in the quiet of the jungle. Birds took flight, their alarmed cries adding to the chaos. Ravi heard the kidnappers shouting to each other, their footsteps moving away from his hiding spot as they ran towards the source of the noise.

For a moment, Ravi allowed himself to feel a glimmer of hope. But as the echoes of the firecrackers faded away, replaced by the angry yells of the kidnappers realizing they had been tricked, that hope dimmed. He was still trapped, still alone, and still no closer to rescuing his brother.

As the reality of his situation sank in, Ravi felt a wave of despair wash over him. What had he been thinking, coming out here on his own? He was no hero, no skilled adventurer. He was just a couch potato who had watched too much TV and foolishly believed he could translate that into real-world skills. His family had been right to doubt him. He wasn't cut out for this.

Ravi slumped against the boulder, his eyes stinging with unshed tears. He thought of his brother, still captive, probably disappointed and angry at Ravi's failed attempt. He thought of his family back home, worried sick and unaware of the danger he had put himself in. He had let them all down.

For a long moment, Ravi sat there, overwhelmed by his failure and fear. The sounds of the jungle seemed to mock him – the rustle of leaves, the distant call of birds, the occasional crack of a branch under the weight of some unseen animal. This world was so far removed from the comfort of his living room couch, from the predictable plots of his favorite shows.

But as he sat there, wallowing in self-pity, something began to stir within him. A voice, small at first but growing stronger, reminded him of why he had embarked on this journey in the first place. He hadn't come all this way, faced so many challenges, just to give up at the first major setback. His brother was still in danger, still counting on him.

Ravi took a deep breath, forcing himself to think rationally. Yes, his first attempt had failed, but that didn't mean all was lost. In fact, he now had valuable information about the kidnappers' hideout and their reactions. He had seen his brother, confirmed he was alive and unharmed. That was more than he had known before.

Slowly, Ravi began to analyze what had gone wrong. He had been too hasty, too confident in his untested abilities. He had underestimated the kidnappers and overestimated himself. But these were mistakes he could learn from. After all, wasn't that what happened in every hero's journey? The protagonist always faced setbacks, moments of doubt and failure. It was how they responded to these challenges that defined them as heroes.

As this realization dawned on him, Ravi felt a renewed sense of determination. He may not be a trained spy or a seasoned jungle survivor, but he had something just as valuable – adaptability. His years of watching diverse TV shows had exposed him to a wealth of ideas and strategies. Now, he needed to apply that knowledge more carefully, more creatively.

Ravi began to formulate a new plan in his mind. This time, he would be more cautious, more thorough in his preparation. He would observe the kidnappers for longer, learn their patterns more intimately. He would prepare multiple backup plans, anticipating potential problems before they arose. And most importantly, he would not let fear drive his actions again.

As the sun began to set, casting long shadows through the trees, Ravi made a silent promise to himself and to his captive brother. He would not fail again. He would find a way to outsmart the kidnappers, to turn his perceived weaknesses into strengths. His journey was far from over, and this setback was just another chapter in the story.

With renewed resolve, Ravi carefully began to move away from his hiding spot. He needed to find a safe place to rest for the night, to gather his strength and refine his plans. Tomorrow would be a new day, a fresh opportunity to prove himself and save his brother.

As he navigated through the darkening jungle, Ravi's mind was already racing with new ideas. He thought about the various survival techniques he had seen on nature documentaries, the clever tricks employed by characters in espionage thrillers. There had to be a way to combine these concepts, to create a strategy that the kidnappers wouldn't expect.

For the first time since his failed rescue attempt, Ravi felt a spark of excitement. This challenge was testing him in ways he never imagined, pushing him to his limits and beyond. But with each obstacle he faced, each problem he solved, he was growing stronger, more capable. The Ravi who had left home, full of naive confidence, was gone. In his place was a more resilient, more determined individual.

As night fell completely, Ravi found a small, sheltered spot to rest. As he settled in, his body aching from the day's exertions, he allowed himself a small smile. Tomorrow was another day, another chance to be the hero his brother needed. And this time, he would be ready.

Chapter 12: The Comeback Kid

As Ravi sat on a rock, his head in his hands, the weight of his failed rescue attempt bore down on him like the oppressive jungle heat. The image of his brother, so close yet still out of reach, haunted his thoughts. But as the sounds of the forest echoed around him, a familiar voice cut through the cacophony – the voice of Bear Grylls, repeating his oft-quoted mantra: "Improvise, adapt, overcome." It was as if the TV survival expert was speaking directly to him, urging him not to give up.

With a deep breath, Ravi lifted his head. He had come too far to surrender now. His brother was counting on him, even if he didn't know it yet. The family back home, who had doubted his abilities, were unknowingly relying on him. He couldn't let them down. He wouldn't let them down.

Ravi stood up, brushing off the debris from his worn clothes. He began to pace, his mind racing through the vast catalog of television shows he had absorbed over the years. Each step brought forth a new idea, a fragment of information that could be useful. It was time to form a new plan, one that would combine all the knowledge he had gained from his countless hours in front of the screen.

First, he thought of the tactical precision he had observed in countless police procedurals. The way detectives meticulously mapped out crime scenes and analyzed every detail. Ravi realized he needed to approach the kidnappers' lair with the same level of attention. He began to sketch a rough map of the area in the dirt, marking the locations of guard posts and potential entry points he had observed during his failed attempt.

As he worked on his makeshift map, a scene from a historical documentary about World War II resistance fighters flashed in his mind. He remembered how they used simple, everyday items to create distractions and sabotage enemy operations. Ravi glanced around at the jungle flora surrounding him, his mind buzzing with possibilities. Perhaps he could use the environment to his advantage, just as those resourceful resistance fighters had done.

The sun began to dip lower in the sky, casting long shadows through the trees. Ravi knew he had to work quickly – nightfall would bring new challenges, but also new opportunities. He recalled an episode of a nature documentary that explained how nocturnal animals navigate in the dark. While he didn't have the benefit of echolocation or enhanced night vision, he could use the cover of darkness to his advantage, just as these creatures did.

As Ravi continued to brainstorm, he found himself drawing inspiration from the most unexpected sources. A cooking show he had once watched on a lazy Sunday afternoon suddenly seemed relevant. The chef had emphasized the importance of mise en place – having all ingredients prepared and ready before starting to cook. Ravi realized he needed to apply the same principle to his rescue mission. He began gathering materials he might need – vines for makeshift ropes, rocks for distractions, leaves for camouflage.

Hours passed as Ravi worked tirelessly, preparing for every contingency he could think of. As the last rays of sunlight disappeared behind the horizon, he felt a renewed sense of purpose and confidence. His plan was coming together, a patchwork of ideas gleaned from years of television viewing, now being put to the ultimate test in the real world.

Ravi couldn't help but chuckle at the irony. All those times his family had chided him for wasting his life in front of the TV, and now that very "waste" might be the key to saving his brother's life. He thought of his parents and how they had always compared him unfavorably to his older sibling. "If only they could see me now," he mused, a small smile playing on his lips.

As he made final preparations, Ravi's mind wandered to an old episode of "MacGyver" he had watched countless times. The resourceful secret agent had always managed to escape seemingly impossible situations with nothing but his wits and whatever materials were at hand. "What would MacGyver do?" Ravi asked himself, scanning his surroundings with newfound purpose.

His eyes fell on a piece of discarded plastic he had been carrying – a remnant of his journey into the jungle. In a flash of inspiration, Ravi remembered how MacGyver had once used a similar piece of plastic to create a makeshift magnifying glass. With trembling hands, he began to shape the plastic, his heart racing with excitement. If this worked, he would have a tool to start a fire silently, providing both a distraction and a potential weapon.

As the night deepened, Ravi's determination grew stronger. He was no longer the couch potato his family believed him to be. He was a man on a mission, armed with a lifetime of accumulated knowledge from the most unlikely of sources. Every challenge he had faced in the jungle so far had only served to prove that he was capable of more than anyone – including himself – had ever imagined.

Ravi took a moment to center himself, closing his eyes and taking deep breaths just as he had seen characters do in countless meditation scenes. He visualized his brother, imagining the look of surprise and relief that would cross his face when Ravi finally reached him. This image steeled his resolve and filled him with a surge of energy.

Opening his eyes, Ravi surveyed his handiwork. Around him lay an array of improvised tools and weapons, each one a testament to his creativity and resourcefulness. He had transformed from a passive observer to an active participant in his own adventure, and the feeling was exhilarating.

As he prepared to put his plan into action, Ravi couldn't help but feel a sense of gratitude for all the hours he had spent glued to the television. What had once been seen as a waste of time had become his lifeline, a vast repository of knowledge that he was now drawing upon to save his brother.

With a final check of his makeshift gear, Ravi stood tall, ready to face whatever challenges lay ahead. He was no longer just Ravi, the couch potato. He was Ravi, the comeback kid, ready to prove to himself, his family, and the world that he was capable of extraordinary things.

As he took his first steps towards the kidnappers' lair, Ravi felt a mix of fear and excitement coursing through his veins. He knew that the path ahead would be fraught with danger, but he also knew that he was as prepared as he could be. With each step, he recited a mantra cobbled together from various motivational speeches he had heard on TV: "I am strong. I am capable. I will succeed."

The jungle seemed to come alive around him, the nocturnal creatures stirring in the darkness. But Ravi moved with a newfound confidence, his senses heightened and alert. He was no longer an outsider in this wild environment but a part of it, using its secrets to his advantage just as he had learned from countless nature documentaries.

As he neared the kidnappers' hideout, Ravi's mind was already racing ahead, planning his next moves. He knew that outsmarting the enemy would require all of his wit and the cumulative knowledge he had gained from years of television viewing. With a deep breath, he steeled himself for the challenges ahead, ready to put his plan into action and prove once and for all that he was more than just a couch potato – he was a hero in the making.

Chapter 13: Outsmarting the Enemy

As we transition from Ravi's moment of doubt and his renewed determination, we now find him ready to put his TV-inspired knowledge to the ultimate test. In this pivotal chapter, Ravi's creativity and quick thinking shine as he prepares to outsmart the kidnappers who hold his brother captive.

The jungle air was thick with tension as Ravi crouched behind a large, moss-covered boulder, his eyes fixed on the kidnappers' hideout. He had spent the last few hours meticulously observing their patterns and routines, channeling the focus of his favorite TV detectives. The kidnappers, a group of four rugged men, seemed to operate with a false sense of security, clearly not expecting anyone to have tracked them this deep into the wilderness.

Ravi's mind raced with ideas, each one inspired by a different TV show he had watched over the years. He thought back to an episode of "MacGyver" where the protagonist had created a diversion using nothing but household items. While Ravi didn't have access to rubber bands or paperclips, he did have the jungle at his disposal. With a determined glint in his eye, he set to work.

First, Ravi gathered a collection of small, round fruits he had noticed growing on nearby trees. These would serve as his "smoke bombs." He carefully punctured each fruit and filled them with a mixture of damp leaves and dry twigs. It wasn't exactly military-grade, but he hoped the smoldering contents would create enough smoke to cause confusion.

Next, inspired by a nature documentary about Amazon tribes, Ravi crafted a rudimentary blow dart using a hollow reed and sharp thorns. He had no intention of actually harming anyone, but the darts, tipped with a harmless but foul-smelling sap he had discovered, would serve as an effective deterrent.

As the sun began to set, casting long shadows across the forest floor, Ravi put the final touches on his most ambitious trap. Using vines and flexible branches, he had constructed a series of trip wires around the perimeter of the hideout. Each wire was connected to a counterweight system that would release a barrage of jungle debris - a combination of rotten fruit, mud, and leaves - onto anyone unfortunate enough to trigger it.

Ravi couldn't help but grin as he surveyed his handiwork. It was like something out of "Home Alone," but with a distinctly tropical twist. He whispered to himself, "Kevin McCallister, eat your heart out."

With his traps set, Ravi waited for the cover of darkness. The jungle came alive with nocturnal sounds, a cacophony of chirps, croaks, and distant howls that seemed to mirror the nervous energy coursing through his veins. He took a deep breath, steeling himself for what was to come. This was it - the moment where all his TV knowledge would be put to the ultimate test.

As the moon rose high in the sky, Ravi made his move. He circled around to the back of the hideout, where he had observed the least activity. With practiced precision, he lit the first of his fruit "smoke bombs" and tossed it near the entrance of the hideout. Within seconds, a plume of acrid smoke began to rise, carrying with it the pungent odor of burning leaves.

The effect was instantaneous. Shouts of confusion erupted from inside the hideout, followed by the sound of hurried footsteps. Ravi quickly lit and threw two more smoke bombs, creating a thick screen of smoke around the building. Through the haze, he could see the kidnappers stumbling out, coughing and disoriented.

It was time for phase two. Ravi raised his makeshift blowgun to his lips and took aim. With a sharp puff of air, he sent the first dart flying, striking one of the kidnappers in the arm. The man yelped in surprise, more startled than hurt, but the foul-smelling sap quickly made its presence known. The kidnapper gagged and stumbled backward, right into one of Ravi's tripwires.

What followed was a scene of utter chaos that would have been right at home in any slapstick comedy. The tripwire triggered its payload, showering the kidnapper with a mixture of rotten fruit and mud. He howled in disgust, flailing wildly and inadvertently setting off two more traps in quick succession. His companions, rushing to his aid, soon found themselves similarly bombarded.

Ravi had to stifle a laugh as he watched the kidnappers, once intimidating figures, now reduced to stumbling, mud-covered forms slipping and sliding in the dark. It was like watching a bizarre jungle version of a pie-throwing contest, and for a moment, Ravi felt a surge of pride in his TV-inspired ingenuity.

But he knew he couldn't afford to get cocky. This was just the diversion he needed to make his way into the hideout and find his brother. As the kidnappers continued to struggle with the traps outside, Ravi slipped silently towards the building, his heart pounding with a mixture of fear and excitement.

The interior of the hideout was dimly lit and sparsely furnished. Ravi moved cautiously, his senses on high alert. He could hear the continued commotion outside, but he knew it was only a matter of time before the kidnappers regained their composure. He had to work fast.

Room by room, Ravi searched, his eyes scanning for any sign of his brother. The first two rooms yielded nothing, but as he approached the third, he heard a muffled sound. His heart leaped into his throat. Could it be?

With trembling hands, Ravi pushed open the door. There, bound to a chair and gagged, but very much alive, was his brother. Their eyes met, and Ravi saw a mixture of disbelief, relief, and confusion flash across his brother's face.

Ravi rushed forward, quickly untying the gag. "It's okay," he whispered, his voice choked with emotion. "I'm here to get you out."

His brother's voice was hoarse as he spoke. "Ravi? How... How did you find me? How did you do all this?"

Ravi managed a small smile as he worked on untying the ropes. "Would you believe me if I said I learned it all from TV?"

Before his brother could respond, they heard angry shouts from outside. The kidnappers had apparently overcome Ravi's traps and were heading back inside. Panic gripped Ravi for a moment, but then a calm determination settled over him. He had come too far to fail now.

"Quick," he said, helping his brother to his feet. "I've got one more trick up my sleeve."

As the kidnappers burst back into the hideout, mud-covered and furious, Ravi and his brother were already making their escape through a back window. The last of Ravi's smoke bombs, strategically placed, provided the cover they needed to disappear into the jungle.

As they ran, ducking under branches and leaping over roots, Ravi's brother looked at him with newfound respect. "I can't believe you did all this," he panted. "When did you become so... capable?"

Ravi grinned, the thrill of success coursing through him. "Let's just say I've been preparing for this my whole life - one episode at a time."

As they put distance between themselves and the hideout, the sounds of the kidnappers' angry shouts fading behind them, Ravi felt a profound sense of accomplishment. He had done it. He had outsmarted the enemy, rescued his brother, and proven to himself that he was capable of far more than anyone - including himself - had ever believed.

The jungle around them seemed to pulse with life, as if celebrating their escape. Ravi knew they weren't out of danger yet - they still had to navigate their way back to civilization. But for the first time since this ordeal began, he felt truly confident. Whatever challenges lay ahead, he was ready to face them.

As they paused to catch their breath, Ravi's brother clasped him on the shoulder. "I don't know how you did it, little brother, but you saved my life. Thank you."

Ravi nodded, emotion welling up in his throat. This adventure was far from over, but he had crossed a threshold. He was no longer the couch potato everyone had dismissed. He was a hero, shaped by the unlikeliest of training grounds - his living room couch and the flickering screen of his television.

As they prepared to continue their journey, Ravi couldn't help but think about what lay ahead. The jungle still held many dangers, and they were far from safe. But with his newfound confidence and the bond forged in this rescue, Ravi felt ready for whatever came next. Little did he know, nature had one final, formidable test in store for them before they could truly claim victory.

Chapter 14: Brother Reunited

As we transition from Ravi's clever maneuvering to outsmart the kidnappers, we now find ourselves at the pivotal moment of reunion between the two brothers. The air is thick with anticipation and emotion as Ravi finally reaches his goal.

Ravi's heart pounded in his chest as he crept through the dimly lit corridor of the kidnappers' hideout. The musty smell of damp earth and stale air filled his nostrils, a stark reminder of how far he had come from the comfort of his living room couch. Every step brought him closer to his brother, yet the weight of uncertainty still pressed upon him. What if he was too late? What if his brother was injured, or worse?

As he approached a heavy wooden door at the end of the corridor, Ravi paused, pressing his ear against the rough surface. He held his breath, straining to hear any sign of life from within. For a moment, there was nothing but silence, and then – a faint shuffling sound. Ravi's pulse quickened. This had to be it.

With trembling hands, Ravi reached for the rusted lock. He fumbled in his pocket for the makeshift lock-picking tools he had fashioned from bits of wire and metal, recalling a late-night marathon of "Escape Artists" that had once seemed like mere entertainment. Now, those hours of passive viewing were proving to be his salvation. Focusing intently, Ravi manipulated the lock mechanism, his brow furrowed in concentration. After what felt like an eternity, but was likely only a minute or two, he heard the satisfying click of the lock disengaging.

Taking a deep breath to steady himself, Ravi slowly pushed the door open. The hinges creaked ominously, and he winced, praying that the sound wouldn't alert any nearby guards. As the gap widened, his eyes struggled to adjust to the darkness within. And then, he saw him.

Huddled in the corner of the small, dank room was a figure that Ravi would recognize anywhere – his brother. Even in the dim light, Ravi could see the mixture of fear and disbelief etched on his brother's face. For a moment, neither of them moved, as if the slightest motion might shatter this fragile reality.

"Ravi?" his brother's voice was barely above a whisper, hoarse from disuse and tinged with uncertainty. "Is that really you?"

The sound of his name broke the spell, and Ravi rushed forward, engulfing his brother in a fierce embrace. "Yes, it's me. I'm here. I've come to get you out," Ravi choked out, his voice thick with emotion.

As they clung to each other, years of sibling rivalry and perceived differences melted away. In that moment, they were simply two brothers, reunited against all odds. Ravi could feel his brother's body shaking, whether from relief, exhaustion, or a combination of both, he couldn't tell.

When they finally pulled apart, Ravi quickly assessed his brother's condition. Despite looking haggard and malnourished, there didn't appear to be any serious injuries. "Can you walk?" Ravi asked, already formulating their escape plan in his mind.

His brother nodded, still seeming dazed by the sudden turn of events. "Ravi, how did you... I mean, what are you doing here? How did you find me?"

Ravi couldn't help but let out a small, nervous laugh. "It's a long story, bro. Let's just say all those hours of watching TV finally paid off."

His brother's eyebrows shot up in surprise, and for a moment, Ravi saw a flicker of the familiar skepticism he'd grown accustomed to over the years. But then, something shifted in his brother's expression – a dawning realization of the enormity of what Ravi had accomplished.

"You came all this way... through the jungle... to rescue me?" his brother asked, his voice filled with a mixture of awe and disbelief.

Ravi nodded, suddenly feeling self-conscious under his brother's scrutiny. "I couldn't just sit at home and do nothing. I had to try."

His brother's eyes welled up with tears, and he gripped Ravi's shoulder tightly. "I always thought... I mean, I never imagined you were capable of something like this. Ravi, I'm sorry. I've underestimated you for so long."

The weight of this admission hung in the air between them. For years, Ravi had lived in his brother's shadow, always seen as the less capable, less ambitious sibling. Now, here they were, roles reversed, with Ravi as the unlikely hero.

"We can talk about all that later," Ravi said, pushing aside the complex emotions stirred by his brother's words. "Right now, we need to focus on getting out of here."

As Ravi helped his brother to his feet, he couldn't help but marvel at the strange twist of fate that had brought them to this moment. All those years of being dismissed as a couch potato, of feeling inferior to his successful older brother, seemed to fall away. In their place was a newfound sense of confidence and purpose.

Ravi quickly filled his brother in on the basics of his plan for escape. As he spoke, he could see the surprise and admiration growing in his brother's eyes. Each detail of Ravi's journey, each clever solution inspired by his vast repository of TV knowledge, seemed to further shatter his brother's preconceived notions about him.

"I can't believe you did all this," his brother said, shaking his head in amazement. "And to think, all those times I told you to stop wasting your life in front of the TV..."

Ravi grinned, despite the gravity of their situation. "Well, I guess sometimes life imitates art. Or in this case, life imitates 'Survivor' and 'MacGyver.'"

As they prepared to make their escape, Ravi felt a surge of determination. The hardest part – finding and reaching his brother – was behind them. Now, they faced the daunting task of escaping the kidnappers' lair and navigating their way back through the treacherous jungle. But for the first time since embarking on this wild rescue mission, Ravi felt truly confident in his abilities.

With one last look around the cramped, dismal room that had been his brother's prison, Ravi took a deep breath. "Ready?" he asked, meeting his brother's gaze.

His brother nodded, a mix of fear and hope in his eyes. "Ready. Lead the way, little brother."

As they stepped out into the corridor, Ravi's mind was already racing, recalling every relevant scene from every action movie and survival show he'd ever watched. The real test was about to begin. But with his brother by his side and his unlikely skillset at the ready, Ravi felt prepared to face whatever challenges lay ahead.

Little did they know, their escape would push them to their limits, testing not only Ravi's unconventional expertise but also the newfound bond between the brothers. As they ventured forth, leaving the room of captivity behind, they were stepping into a new chapter of their relationship – one forged in the fires of adversity and mutual respect.

The corridor stretched before them, dark and foreboding. Ravi's ears strained for any sound of approaching danger as they moved silently forward. His brother followed close behind, still weak from his ordeal but fueled by the hope of freedom. Every step brought them closer to safety, but also increased the risk of discovery.

As they navigated the labyrinthine passages of the hideout, Ravi's mind raced through countless scenarios he'd seen played out on screen. He found himself drawing on the stealth techniques of spies, the problem-solving skills of detectives, and the survival instincts of wilderness experts. It was as if his years of passive viewing had prepared him for this very moment, transforming him from a couch potato into a real-life action hero.

They encountered their first major obstacle at a junction where two corridors met. Voices drifted from around the corner, growing louder with each passing second. Ravi's heart raced as he frantically searched for a solution. Then, like a bolt of lightning, a scene from an old heist movie flashed in his mind.

"Quick," he whispered to his brother, "help me with this."

Together, they pried loose a section of rusty pipe from the wall. As the voices drew nearer, Ravi positioned the pipe across the corridor at ankle height. Then, pulling his brother into a shadowy alcove, they waited with bated breath.

The unsuspecting kidnappers rounded the corner, engrossed in conversation. In a matter of seconds, they stumbled over the pipe, crashing to the ground with shouts of surprise and pain. Before the men could regain their footing, Ravi and his brother were already sprinting down the opposite corridor, their footsteps masked by the commotion behind them.

As they ran, Ravi's brother shot him a look of astonishment. "Where did you learn to do that?" he panted.

Ravi couldn't help but smile, despite the danger. "Let's just say George Clooney and Brad Pitt are pretty good teachers."

This daring escape was just the beginning of their harrowing journey out of the kidnappers' lair. Each new challenge they faced seemed to further cement the growing respect between the brothers. Ravi's quick thinking and unconventional solutions repeatedly saved them from detection and capture, while his brother's physical strength and endurance – honed by years of conventional success – complemented Ravi's skills perfectly.

As they finally emerged from the hideout into the dense jungle beyond, both brothers were breathing heavily, equal parts exhausted and exhilarated. The warm, humid air of the forest was a stark contrast to the stale atmosphere of captivity, and Ravi's brother took a moment to simply breathe it in, savoring his newfound freedom.

"I can't believe we made it," he said, turning to Ravi with a mix of gratitude and admiration. "I owe you my life, little brother."

Ravi felt a warmth spread through his chest at these words. For so long, he had yearned for his brother's approval, always feeling like he fell short. Now, standing in the heart of the jungle, covered in dirt and scrapes but filled with a sense of accomplishment, Ravi realized that he had finally earned not just his brother's approval, but his respect.

"We're not out of the woods yet," Ravi replied, both literally and figuratively. "We've still got a long journey ahead of us."

His brother nodded, a new determination settling over his features. "Then let's face it together. I have a feeling I've got a lot to learn from you, Ravi."

As they set off into the dense foliage, Ravi felt a shift in their dynamic. No longer was he the lazy younger brother, forever in the shadow of success. He had proven himself capable, resourceful, and brave. And more importantly, he had discovered strengths within himself that he never knew existed.

The jungle loomed before them, full of unknown dangers and challenges. But as Ravi led the way, drawing on his vast mental library of survival tips and adventure scenarios, he felt ready for whatever lay ahead. With his brother by his side and a newfound confidence in his abilities, Ravi knew that this was just the beginning of their great escape.

As they ventured deeper into the wild, leaving the kidnappers' lair behind, both brothers were acutely aware that their ordeal was far from over. The dense jungle presented a new set of challenges, ones that would test their physical endurance, mental fortitude, and the strength of their newly forged bond. Little did they know, nature had one last, formidable test in store for them before they could truly taste freedom.

Chapter 15: The Great Escape

As Ravi and his brother emerged from the kidnappers' lair, the overwhelming sense of relief was quickly replaced by a surge of adrenaline. They knew their journey was far from over. The dense jungle that had been Ravi's nemesis and ally for the past days now stood as their only hope for escape. With the sounds of angry shouts and hurried footsteps growing behind them, the brothers exchanged a quick glance before plunging into the thick foliage.

Ravi's mind raced as he led the way, drawing upon every scrap of knowledge he had gleaned from countless hours of survival shows. He recalled an episode where the host had emphasized the importance of breaking one's trail to throw off pursuers. "This way," he whispered urgently to his brother, veering sharply to the left and stepping carefully on rocks and fallen logs to minimize their tracks.

The undergrowth was dense, branches whipping at their faces and vines threatening to ensnare their feet with every step. Ravi's brother, weak from his captivity, stumbled frequently. Each time, Ravi would pause, his heart pounding, to help his sibling up. The irony wasn't lost on him – the brother who had always been the family's pride was now relying on the perceived failure for survival.

As they pushed deeper into the jungle, the sounds of pursuit began to fade, but Ravi knew better than to slow their pace. He had watched enough crime dramas to understand that the first few hours of an escape were crucial. "We need to put as much distance between us and them as possible," he panted, helping his brother over a fallen tree.

The jungle, which had seemed so hostile during Ravi's initial journey, now felt like a protective cloak. The thick canopy above shielded them from aerial detection, while the cacophony of wildlife masked the sound of their labored breathing and snapping twigs underfoot. Ravi found himself silently thanking the countless nature documentaries that had familiarized him with this environment.

As they pressed on, Ravi's brother began to falter. "I... I need to rest," he gasped, leaning heavily against a tree trunk. Ravi's instinct was to keep moving, but he knew they needed to pace themselves. He quickly scanned their surroundings, recalling a technique he'd seen on a wilderness survival show.

"Okay, but not here," Ravi replied, guiding his brother to a small clearing nearby. "We'll rest, but we need to cover our tracks." He demonstrated how to use a leafy branch to sweep away their footprints, working backwards until they reached the clearing. It was a tedious process, but one that could mean the difference between freedom and recapture.

As they caught their breath, Ravi's brother looked at him with a mix of exhaustion and amazement. "How do you know all this stuff?" he asked between gulps of air. Ravi couldn't help but smile wryly. "TV," he replied simply, earning a disbelieving chuckle from his sibling.

Their respite was short-lived. A distant shout jolted them back to the reality of their situation. "They're getting closer," Ravi muttered, his mind racing. He needed a plan, something to throw their pursuers off the scent. Suddenly, an episode of a crime show flashed in his mind – one where the fugitives had used a river to mask their trail.

"Do you hear that?" Ravi asked, straining his ears. The faint sound of rushing water reached them, barely audible over the jungle's ambient noise. "There's a river nearby. If we can reach it, we can use it to throw them off."

With renewed urgency, the brothers set off towards the sound of water. The terrain became more treacherous as they approached the river, the ground growing steep and slippery. Ravi's brother slipped, nearly falling down the incline, but Ravi's quick reflexes – honed by years of video games – allowed him to grab his sibling's arm just in time.

When they finally reached the riverbank, both were panting heavily. The water rushed by, fast and frothy, presenting a new challenge. Ravi's mind flicked through various TV shows, searching for any information on river crossings. He recalled a documentary about indigenous tribes in the Amazon, where they had used vines as makeshift ropes to cross turbulent waters.

"We need to find some strong vines," Ravi explained, already scanning the nearby trees. His brother, still catching his breath, nodded weakly. They worked quickly, Ravi testing the strength of various vines while his brother kept watch.

As they prepared to cross, a noise from upstream made them freeze. The kidnappers were close – too close. In a split-second decision, Ravi grabbed a large branch from the ground. "Get in the water," he whispered urgently to his brother. "Hold onto this branch and let the current carry you downstream. I'll be right behind you."

His brother hesitated, fear evident in his eyes. This was the moment of truth – would he trust Ravi, the brother he had always seen as incompetent? Time seemed to stand still as their eyes met. Then, with a nod, his brother slipped into the water, clinging to the branch.

Ravi quickly followed, the shock of the cold water momentarily taking his breath away. The current was stronger than he had anticipated, threatening to tear the branch from their grasp. But Ravi held firm, drawing strength from every action movie river scene he had ever watched.

As they were swept downstream, Ravi could hear shouts of frustration from the bank. The kidnappers had reached the river, but the brothers were already out of sight, carried around a bend by the swift current. For the first time since their escape began, Ravi allowed himself a small smile. They were going to make it.

The river carried them for what felt like hours, though Ravi knew it couldn't have been more than twenty minutes. When the current finally began to slow, he guided them towards the bank, helping his exhausted brother out of the water.

As they collapsed on the riverbank, soaked and shivering but alive, Ravi's brother turned to him with newfound respect in his eyes. "I never thought I'd say this," he panted, "but thank God for your TV addiction."

Ravi couldn't help but laugh, the sound echoing through the jungle. It was a moment of levity in their dire situation, a brief respite from the fear and tension that had gripped them. But Ravi knew they couldn't afford to relax just yet. Their journey was far from over.

As they caught their breath and wrung out their soaked clothes, Ravi's mind was already racing ahead to their next move. The river had bought them some time and distance, but they were still deep in unfamiliar territory, with unknown dangers lurking in every shadow.

Ravi knew that their survival now depended on more than just evading their pursuers. They would need to navigate through the jungle, find food and water, and somehow make their way back to civilization. It was a daunting task, but as Ravi looked at his brother – the sibling who had always seemed so much more capable than him – he felt a surge of determination.

For the first time in his life, Ravi was the one with the knowledge and skills they needed to survive. All those hours spent in front of the TV, which his family had dismissed as wasted time, were now proving to be their salvation. As they prepared to continue their journey, Ravi silently vowed to get them both home safely, no matter what challenges lay ahead.

With renewed purpose, Ravi helped his brother to his feet. "We need to keep moving," he said, his voice steady with newfound confidence. "I think I know how we can find our way out of here." As they set off once more into the depths of the jungle, Ravi couldn't help but feel a mix of fear and excitement. The greatest test of his unconventional knowledge still lay ahead, and he was determined to prove that sometimes, being a couch potato could save your life.

Chapter 16: Nature's Last Test

As Ravi and his brother emerged from the dense undergrowth, their hearts pounding with a mixture of exhaustion and exhilaration, they were met with an unexpected sight. Before them stretched a raging river, its waters swollen from recent rains and churning with a ferocity that seemed to mock their hopes of an easy escape. The brothers exchanged a glance, both recognizing that this was nature's final test before they could reach safety.

Ravi took a deep breath, his mind racing through the countless hours of nature documentaries he had watched. He remembered a particular episode about the salmon run, where the fish battled against powerful currents to reach their spawning grounds. The narrator's voice echoed in his head, describing the importance of finding the right moment and the right spot to make the crossing.

"We can't cross here," Ravi said, his voice steady despite the fatigue that weighed on him. "The current's too strong. We need to find a wider, shallower part of the river." His brother nodded, trusting Ravi's judgment that had brought them this far.

They began to move upstream, carefully picking their way along the rocky bank. Ravi's eyes scanned the water, looking for telltale signs of a safer crossing point. As they walked, he explained to his brother what he was searching for, sharing the knowledge he had gleaned from hours of television viewing that now seemed like preparation for this very moment.

"See how the water's white and foamy there?" Ravi pointed to a particularly turbulent section. "That means there are rocks just below the surface. We want to avoid those areas. We're looking for a place where the water is moving, but not too fast, and where we can see the bottom."

His brother listened intently, amazed at Ravi's expertise. "I had no idea you knew so much about rivers," he said, a note of admiration in his voice. Ravi felt a surge of pride, realizing that for the first time in his life, his older brother was looking to him for guidance.

As they continued their search, Ravi's mind drifted to a survival show he had watched religiously. The host had demonstrated how to cross a river safely, emphasizing the importance of teamwork. "When we find a good spot," Ravi explained, "we'll need to link arms. It'll help us stay stable against the current."

After what seemed like hours but was likely only twenty minutes, they found a promising location. The river widened here, its flow less frenzied. Ravi could make out the riverbed through the water, which was a good sign. He took a moment to study the current, looking for the safest path across.

"Okay, this is it," Ravi announced, his voice a mixture of determination and nervousness. "Remember, we stay together. If one of us slips, the other needs to hold on tight." His brother nodded, his face set with resolve.

They removed their shoes, tying the laces together and draping them around their necks. Ravi knew from his TV shows that wet shoes would be heavy and could drag them down. He also recalled an episode where the host had emphasized the importance of keeping one's center of gravity low when crossing swift water.

"We'll need to face upstream," Ravi instructed. "And we'll move sideways, one step at a time. Don't try to fight the current directly; just focus on moving across."

They linked arms and stepped into the water. The cold shocked Ravi's system, nearly causing him to gasp. He remembered another tip from his survival shows: control your breathing to maintain calm. He took deep, measured breaths, feeling his brother do the same beside him.

As they moved deeper, the current grew stronger, pushing against their legs with increasing force. Ravi felt his brother's grip tighten on his arm, and he returned the pressure, silently communicating his support. They moved slowly, each step careful and deliberate.

Halfway across, Ravi's foot slipped on a smooth stone. For a heart-stopping moment, he felt himself being pulled downstream. But his brother's firm grip kept him upright, and Ravi quickly regained his footing. They paused for a moment, catching their breath and steadying themselves.

"You okay?" his brother asked, concern evident in his voice.

Ravi nodded, managing a small smile. "Yeah, thanks to you. We're a team, remember?"

As they continued their crossing, Ravi felt a newfound respect blooming between them. This shared challenge, this moment of mutual reliance, was forging a bond stronger than any they had known before. Despite the danger, despite the cold water numbing their legs, Ravi felt a warmth in his chest.

Finally, after what seemed like an eternity, they reached the opposite bank. Climbing out of the water, they collapsed on the shore, breathing heavily but grinning with the triumph of their accomplishment. They had faced nature's last test together and emerged victorious.

As they sat catching their breath, Ravi's brother turned to him with a look of genuine admiration. "Ravi, I... I don't know what to say. You've been incredible throughout this whole ordeal. I never knew you had all this in you."

Ravi felt a surge of emotion at his brother's words. For years, he had lived in his sibling's shadow, always feeling inadequate in comparison. Now, here they were, equals in this adventure, each bringing their own strengths to the table.

"I guess all those hours in front of the TV weren't wasted after all," Ravi jokes, but there was a note of pride in his voice.

His brother chuckled, shaking his head in amazement. "I'll never underestimate the power of educational programming again. But Ravi, it's not just the knowledge. It's how you've applied it, how you've stepped up when it mattered most. You're braver and more capable than I ever gave you credit for."

As they sat there, the sound of the river a constant backdrop to their conversation, Ravi felt a shift in their relationship. The admiration in his brother's eyes, the genuine respect in his voice – these were things Ravi had always craved but never expected to receive. He realized that this journey had not only been about rescuing his brother but also about discovering his own potential.

"We should get moving," Ravi said after a while, his practical side taking over. "We're not out of danger yet."

His brother nodded, getting to his feet. As they prepared to continue their journey, now on the home stretch towards safety, Ravi felt a new confidence in his step. He had faced the jungle, outsmarted kidnappers, and conquered a raging river. Whatever challenges lay ahead, he knew he was ready to face them.

As they set off, leaving the river behind them, Ravi's thoughts turned to what awaited them beyond the jungle. He knew that once they reached safety, once the immediate danger had passed, they would face a different kind of challenge. They would need to recount their ordeal to their family and the authorities, a prospect that filled Ravi with a mix of anticipation and apprehension.

How would he explain the source of his survival knowledge? Would anyone believe that his countless hours of watching nature documentaries and survival shows had actually prepared him for this real-life adventure? As they walked, Ravi began to imagine the scene of their return, picturing the looks of disbelief on his family's faces as he recounted their journey.

But those thoughts were for later. For now, they had to focus on the final leg of their escape. The jungle was still thick around them, but Ravi could sense a change in the air. The vegetation seemed less dense, the animal sounds more distant. They were nearing the edge of the wilderness, closer to civilization with every step.

As they pushed forward, Ravi and his brother shared a comfortable silence, broken only by the occasional comment about their surroundings or a word of encouragement. The bond between them had deepened through their shared ordeal, transforming their relationship in ways that would last long after this adventure was over.

With the river crossing behind them and safety within reach, Ravi allowed himself a moment of reflection. He had entered this jungle as the family's perceived underachiever, the couch potato with no real-world skills. Now, as they neared the end of their journey, he emerged as someone entirely different – a resourceful, courageous individual capable of facing incredible challenges.

As the jungle began to thin and the first signs of human habitation appeared in the distance, Ravi felt a mix of relief and nostalgia. Despite the dangers and hardships, this adventure had awakened something in him, a spark of confidence and capability that he never knew he possessed. Whatever awaited them beyond the jungle's edge, Ravi knew that he was returning a changed man, ready to face the world with newfound strength and self-assurance.

Chapter 17: Out of the Woods

As Ravi and his brother emerged from the dense foliage of the jungle, the stark contrast between the wild terrain they had just traversed and the organized civilization before them was almost jarring. The brothers stumbled onto a dirt road, their clothes tattered and their bodies bearing the marks of their harrowing journey. Ravi's eyes, now accustomed to the dappled light filtering through the canopy, squinted against the harsh sunlight of the open space. His brother, still weak from his ordeal with the kidnappers, leaned heavily on Ravi's shoulder.

The sound of an approaching vehicle broke the relative silence, and Ravi tensed, his mind immediately racing through the various scenarios he had seen play out in crime dramas. But as the battered pickup truck came into view, he saw the familiar insignia of the local police force emblazoned on its side. Relief washed over him, and he raised his free arm, waving it frantically to catch the driver's attention.

The truck screeched to a halt, kicking up a cloud of dust that momentarily obscured the brothers from view. As it settled, two officers jumped out, their expressions a mix of shock and disbelief. "Are you Ravi and Arjun Sharma?" one of them asked, his voice tinged with urgency and hope. Ravi nodded, his throat too dry and emotions too raw to form words. The officers rushed forward, supporting Arjun and guiding both brothers to the vehicle.

As they drove towards the nearest town, Ravi's mind swirled with a cacophony of thoughts and emotions. The adrenaline that had fueled him throughout their escape began to ebb, leaving him feeling drained and somewhat disoriented. He glanced at his brother, who had fallen into an exhausted sleep, his head lolling against the window. A surge of protectiveness washed over Ravi, surprising him with its intensity.

This was a new feeling, one that had been forged in the crucible of their shared ordeal.

The journey to their hometown seemed to pass in a blur. Ravi found himself drifting in and out of consciousness, the gentle rumble of the truck pulling him into a state of semi-sleep. Images from their adventure flashed behind his closed eyelids – the dense jungle, the face of the kidnapper he had outwitted, the moment he had first laid eyes on Arjun in that makeshift prison. Each memory was tinged with a surreal quality, as if it belonged to someone else's life, not the couch potato he had been just days ago.

As they approached their neighborhood, Ravi felt a knot forming in his stomach. How would his family react? Would they believe what had happened? Would they finally see him as more than just a lazy, TV-obsessed disappointment? The questions swirled in his mind, adding to the surreal nature of the moment.

The police truck pulled up in front of their modest home, and Ravi saw a flurry of movement through the windows. Before the vehicle had even come to a complete stop, the front door burst open, and his parents rushed out, followed closely by his sister and a few neighbors who had been keeping vigil with the family.

The moment Ravi stepped out of the truck, supporting a still-groggy Arjun, time seemed to stand still. For a heartbeat, there was absolute silence as his family took in the sight before them – their sons, whom they had feared lost forever, standing there, battered but alive. Then, as if a dam had burst, they surged forward with cries of joy and disbelief.

Ravi's mother reached them first, her hands trembling as she touched their faces, as if to confirm that they were real and not some cruel apparition. "My boys," she whispered, tears streaming down her face. "My precious boys." She pulled them both into a fierce embrace, and

Ravi felt his own eyes welling up with tears he hadn't allowed himself to shed throughout the entire ordeal.

His father, usually a stoic man, was openly weeping as he joined the embrace. Ravi felt the strong arms of his father encircling them all, and for a moment, he was transported back to his childhood, when those same arms had made him feel safe and protected. Now, as an adult who had faced unimaginable dangers, he found that the feeling of security in his father's embrace hadn't diminished one bit.

As the family slowly disentangled themselves, Ravi noticed the look of utter astonishment on his sister's face. Priya had always been the one to tease him most about his TV habits, dubbing him the family's resident couch potato. Now, she stared at him with a mixture of awe and confusion, as if seeing him for the first time. "Ravi," she said, her voice barely above a whisper, "how did you... what happened?"

Before Ravi could respond, a commotion at the edge of the gathering caught everyone's attention. The local media, alerted by the police, had arrived en masse. Cameras flashed, and reporters shouted questions, creating a chaotic backdrop to the family's emotional reunion.

Ravi's father, ever the protector, quickly ushered the family inside, away from the prying eyes of the media. As they entered the familiar confines of their living room, Ravi was struck by how unchanged everything was. The same worn sofa where he had spent countless hours watching TV, the same faded curtains, the same family photos on the walls. Yet, he felt like a stranger in this once-familiar space.

As Arjun was gently lowered onto the sofa, their mother fussing over him and checking for visible injuries, Ravi found himself the center of attention. His father, having regained some of his composure, looked at him with a mixture of pride and bewilderment. "Son," he began, his voice hoarse with emotion, "we need to know what happened. How did you find Arjun? How did you both escape?"

Ravi took a deep breath, suddenly feeling the weight of his experiences pressing down on him. How could he possibly explain the journey he had undertaken, both physically and emotionally? How could he convey the fear, the determination, the moments of doubt and triumph that had shaped him over the past days?

As he opened his mouth to speak, he caught sight of the television in the corner of the room. The irony wasn't lost on him – this object, once his constant companion and escape, now seemed like a relic from another life. Yet, it was the very knowledge he had gained from his countless hours in front of that screen that had saved both his and Arjun's lives.

"It's a long story," Ravi began, his voice steady despite the tumult of emotions within him. "And you might find some parts hard to believe." He paused, looking around at the faces of his family, seeing the mix of love, concern, and curiosity in their eyes. "But I promise you, every word is true."

As Ravi began to recount his incredible journey, he could see the expressions on his family's faces change from disbelief to amazement. He told them about his decision to go after Arjun, despite everyone's doubts. He described the challenges he faced in the jungle, and how he had used knowledge gleaned from nature documentaries and survival shows to overcome them.

His sister gasped when he spoke about his close call with the kidnappers, and how he had used camouflage techniques he'd seen on a military documentary to avoid detection. His mother's eyes widened as he recounted his encounter with the local who had helped him, and how he had navigated cultural differences using insights from travel shows.

Throughout his narrative, Ravi could see his father's expression shifting from skepticism to pride. When he described how he had outsmarted the kidnappers using strategies inspired by heist movies, his father actually chuckled, shaking his head in wonder.

As Ravi's tale neared its conclusion, he felt a hand on his arm. He turned to see Arjun, who had been listening silently, his eyes filled with gratitude and a new respect for his younger brother. "I never thought I'd say this," Arjun said, his voice weak but filled with emotion, "but all those hours you spent watching TV... they saved my life. They saved both our lives."

The room fell silent as the weight of Arjun's words sank in. Ravi felt a warmth spreading through his chest, a feeling of acceptance and validation he had never experienced before. His mother, tears once again streaming down her face, pulled him into another embrace. "My brave, clever boy," she murmured. "I'm so sorry we ever doubted you."

As the day wore on, more people arrived at the house – relatives, friends, and eventually, police officers who needed to make official statements. Through it all, Ravi found himself repeatedly retelling his story, each time marveling at the reality of what he had accomplished.

The local news crew, persistent in their pursuit of the story, were finally granted a brief interview. As Ravi stood in front of the camera, he felt a strange mix of nervousness and confidence. The reporter, eager for a sensational angle, asked, "How does it feel to be a real-life hero?"

Ravi paused, considering the question. "I don't know if I'm a hero," he said finally. "I just did what I had to do to save my brother. And I couldn't have done it without all the knowledge I gained from years of watching TV. I guess you could say I'm living proof that not all screen time is wasted time."

As evening fell and the excitement began to die down, Ravi found a moment of quiet on the front porch. He sat on the steps, looking out at the street where he had played as a child, marveling at how different everything looked through his new eyes.

He heard the door open behind him and turned to see his father step out, two steaming cups of chai in his hands. Wordlessly, he handed one to Ravi and sat down beside him. For a while, they sat in companionable silence, sipping their tea and watching the stars emerge in the darkening sky.

Finally, his father spoke. "You know, Ravi," he began, his voice thoughtful, "I've spent years worrying about you. About your future, your potential. I thought all that time you spent in front of the TV was holding you back." He paused, taking another sip of his chai. "I've never been so happy to be proven wrong."

Ravi felt a lump form in his throat. "Dad, I-"

His father held up a hand, silencing him gently. "Let me finish, son. What you did... It was extraordinary. Not just the bravery and the cleverness, though those were impressive enough. But the way you took something we all thought was a weakness and turned it into a strength. That's... that's something special."

Ravi nodded, unable to speak past the emotion clogging his throat. His father continued, "I want you to know that whatever you choose to do from here on out, whatever path you decide to take, your mother and I will support you. Because you've shown us that you have the ability to make the most of any situation, to find value where others might not see it."

As the night deepened around them, father and son sat side by side, their relationship forever changed by the events of the past days. Ravi knew that tomorrow would bring new challenges – dealing with the aftermath of the kidnapping, facing the media, deciding what to do with his newfound skills and confidence. But for now, he was content to sit in this moment, savoring the warmth of his father's acceptance and the knowledge that he had forever altered the course of his life.

Inside the house, the TV sat silent, no longer the center of Ravi's universe. But as he contemplated his future, he knew that he would never again underestimate the power of knowledge, no matter where it came from. The world had opened up to him in ways he had never imagined, and he was eager to explore it – both on screen and off.

As Ravi and his father finally stood to go back inside, they were greeted by the sight of Arjun, supported by their mother, making his way to the porch. "Room for two more?" Arjun asked with a weak smile. Ravi and his father made space, and soon the whole family was seated together, looking out at the quiet street.

In this moment of peace, surrounded by the family he had risked everything to protect, Ravi felt a profound sense of belonging. He had left this porch days ago as a boy lost in fictional worlds, and he had returned as a man who had created his own real-life adventure. As he looked at the faces of his loved ones, illuminated by the soft glow of the porch light, he knew that this was just the beginning of a new chapter in his life.

The events of the past days had shown him that he was capable of far more than he, or anyone else, had ever imagined. And while the jungle adventure was over, Ravi knew that the greatest journey – that of discovering his true potential and place in the world – was just beginning. With his family's support and his newfound confidence, he was ready to face whatever challenges lay ahead, both on and off the screen.

Chapter 18: The Hero's Tale

As we transition from the emotional reunion of Ravi and his brother with their worried family, we now delve into the aftermath of their harrowing adventure. The initial shock and disbelief that greeted their return gradually give way to curiosity and amazement as Ravi begins to recount his tale.

Seated in the familiar living room, surrounded by his family and local authorities, Ravi finds himself at the center of attention - a stark contrast to his usual position as the overlooked couch potato. The television, once his constant companion, now sits silent in the background, its screens dark as all eyes focus on the unlikely hero.

Ravi clears his throat, his voice slightly hoarse from days in the jungle. "It all started when I heard about the kidnapping," he begins, his words hesitant at first but gradually gaining confidence. As he speaks, the room falls into a hushed silence, hanging on every word of his incredible journey.

He describes his initial decision to embark on the rescue mission, earning looks of astonishment from his parents. Their expressions of disbelief mirror their earlier skepticism when Ravi first announced his intentions to save his brother. Now, as they listen to the details of his preparation and departure, their faces begin to show the first hints of pride and admiration.

Ravi's narrative takes on a life of its own as he recounts his first steps into the unknown jungle. His description of applying survival skills learned from "Man vs. Wild" elicits a mix of gasps and chuckles from his audience. The local police officer listening to the tale raises an eyebrow, clearly impressed by Ravi's resourcefulness.

As Ravi delves into the challenges he faced, his voice grows more animated. He gesticulated wildly, mimicking his actions as he describes how he overcame each obstacle. His family leans forward, captivated by the transformation of their once-passive son and brother into a man of action and quick thinking.

The room erupts in laughter as Ravi recounts his humorous cultural misunderstandings with the locals who helped him. His self-deprecating humor and ability to laugh at his own mistakes endear him further to his listeners. Even the stern-faced detective taking notes can't suppress a smile at Ravi's animated retelling.

Tension fills the air as Ravi describes his close calls with the kidnappers. His parents clutch each other's hands, reliving the fear and worry they experienced during his absence. His brother, seated beside him, nods in agreement, adding occasional comments to corroborate Ravi's story.

The mood shifts as Ravi talks about his moments of doubt and fear. His voice softens, revealing the vulnerability beneath his newfound bravery. "There were times I thought I couldn't do it," he admits, his eyes downcast. "But then I'd remember something I'd seen on TV, and it would give me the push I needed to keep going."

This confession draws murmurs of sympathy and encouragement from his listeners. His mother reaches out to squeeze his hand, her eyes brimming with tears of pride and love. It's a poignant moment that underscores the depth of Ravi's transformation and the emotional journey his family has undergone.

As Ravi describes the final rescue and escape, excitement builds in his voice. He stands up, acting out parts of the story, his earlier hesitation completely gone. His brother joins in, the two of them recreating their teamwork for their rapt audience. Their synchronized movements and shared glances speak volumes about the bond forged through their shared ordeal.

Throughout his tale, Ravi peppers his narrative with references to the TV shows and documentaries that inspired his actions. What once seemed like useless trivia has become life-saving knowledge in Ravi's hands. The irony is not lost on his family, who exchange looks of amazement at how their son's perceived weakness became his greatest strength.

As Ravi's story winds down, the atmosphere in the room is charged with a mix of emotions. Relief at the safe return of both brothers, awe at Ravi's unexpected capabilities, and a newfound respect for the young man they had underestimated for so long.

The police officer clears his throat, breaking the spell cast by Ravi's narrative. "That's quite a tale, young man," he says, his tone a mix of admiration and lingering disbelief. "We'll need to verify some details, of course, but if everything checks out, you've done an incredible thing."

Ravi nods, understanding the need for official corroboration. He turns to his brother, seeking confirmation. "It's all true," his brother affirms, his voice filled with gratitude and newfound respect. "Every word of it. Ravi saved my life."

These words hang in the air, their weight palpable. Ravi's parents exchange a look, years of assumptions and misconceptions crumbling in the face of this new reality. Their once-dismissed son now sits before them, transformed into a hero.

As the initial excitement settles, questions begin to pour in. Family members and authorities alike are eager to understand more about Ravi's journey. How did he navigate the jungle? How did he outsmart the kidnappers? Where did he find the courage to face such dangers?

Ravi answers each question with a mix of humility and pride. He credits his TV knowledge but also acknowledges the inner strength he discovered along the way. "I guess I always had it in me," he reflects, a note of wonder in his voice. "I just needed the right motivation to bring it out."

This statement resonates with everyone in the room. It's a powerful reminder of the potential that lies dormant within us all, waiting for the right circumstances to emerge. Ravi's story is not just one of rescue and adventure, but of self-discovery and personal growth.

As the questioning continues, Ravi's family begins to see him in a new light. The transformation is evident not just in the story he tells, but in the way he carries himself. Gone is the slouch of the couch potato, replaced by the confident posture of someone who has faced his fears and emerged victorious.

His parents, in particular, seem to be grappling with this new version of their son. Their expressions fluctuate between pride, amazement, and a touch of guilt for having underestimated him for so long. It's clear that Ravi's adventure has not only changed him but will also reshape the dynamics of the entire family.

As the evening wears on, the official part of the questioning comes to an end. The authorities thank Ravi for his cooperation and courage, promising to follow up on the information he's provided about the kidnappers. As they leave, there's a sense that Ravi's story will become the stuff of local legend.

With the officials gone, the atmosphere in the room relaxes. Ravi's extended family members take turns hugging him, expressing their relief and admiration. There's a festive air as someone suggests ordering food to celebrate the safe return of both brothers.

Amidst the bustle, Ravi finds a quiet moment with his parents. His father, a man of few words, places a hand on Ravi's shoulder. "I'm proud of you, son," he says simply, his voice gruff with emotion. His mother, tears in her eyes, pulls him into a tight embrace. No words are needed to convey the depth of her love and newfound respect.

As the night progresses, the initial awe of Ravi's tale begins to give way to a sense of normalcy. Yet, it's a new normal, one where Ravi is no longer the family's underachiever but a source of pride and inspiration. The TV, once Ravi's constant companion, remains off, a silent testament to the real-life adventure that has unfolded.

As the family gathering winds down and people begin to leave, there's a sense of anticipation in the air. Ravi's story has captivated everyone who's heard it, and it's clear that word will spread quickly. Tomorrow will bring new challenges - dealing with media attention, following up with the authorities, and navigating his newfound status as a local hero.

But for now, Ravi is content to bask in the warmth of his family's love and admiration. As he heads to bed, exhausted but exhilarated, he catches a glimpse of himself in the mirror. The person staring back at him is not the same couch potato who left on a seemingly impossible mission. He's someone new - confident, capable, and ready to face whatever challenges life might bring.

As Ravi drifts off to sleep, his mind is already turning to the future. His adventure has opened up a world of possibilities, and he's eager to explore them. But that's a story for another day. For now, he's happy to have found his place in the family and in the world, no longer lost in the glow of the TV screen but shining with his own inner light.

As we conclude this chapter of Ravi's incredible journey, we stand on the cusp of a new beginning. The aftermath of his heroic rescue has set the stage for significant changes in Ravi's life and his family's perception of him. In the next chapter, we'll explore how these changes manifest and the new perspective that emerges from this transformative experience.

124

Chapter 19: A New Perspective

As we move from the thrilling escape and emotional reunion of the previous chapter, we now turn our attention to the aftermath of Ravi's incredible journey. The dust has settled, and the reality of what transpired in the jungle is slowly sinking in for both Ravi and his family. This chapter explores the profound changes that have taken place, not just in how Ravi's family perceives him, but in how Ravi sees himself and his potential.

The days following Ravi and his brother's return were a whirlwind of activity. Media attention, police inquiries, and concerned relatives all descended upon the family home. Amidst this chaos, a subtle but significant shift was taking place within the family dynamic. Gone were the dismissive glances and exasperated sighs that once greeted Ravi's presence. Instead, his parents and siblings watched him with a mixture of awe, pride, and a touch of guilt for their previous misconceptions.

Ravi's mother, who had once lamented her son's apparent lack of ambition, now found herself defending him fiercely to curious neighbors and relatives. "You don't know my Ravi," she would say, her voice swelling with pride. "He's not just smart from all those TV shows he watches. He's brave and resourceful. He saved his brother's life!" The transformation in her attitude was palpable, and Ravi felt a warmth in his chest every time he overheard these conversations.

His father, a man of few words, struggled to express the newfound respect he held for his younger son. One evening, as Ravi sat quietly reading a book – a new habit he had developed since his return – his father approached him. With a hand on Ravi's shoulder, he simply said, "You've made me proud, son. More than you know." The weight of those words, coming from a man who had always seemed disappointed in Ravi, was almost overwhelming. Ravi felt a lump form in his throat as he nodded in acknowledgment, unable to speak.

Perhaps the most significant change was in Ravi's relationship with his rescued brother. Once distant and often condescending, his brother now looked at Ravi with a mixture of gratitude and admiration. The shared ordeal had forged a bond between them that went beyond mere sibling obligation. They spent hours talking, with Ravi's brother eager to understand every detail of the rescue mission. "I still can't believe you did all that," he would say, shaking his head in wonder. "And to think, all those hours of watching TV actually paid off!"

This newfound closeness extended to shared activities as well. Ravi's brother, once too busy with his successful career to spend time with his "lazy" younger sibling, now made a point of including Ravi in his life. They went on hikes together, with Ravi proudly pointing out various plants and their uses, knowledge gleaned from countless nature documentaries. His brother listened with genuine interest, seeing his younger sibling in a completely new light.

As the family's perception of Ravi evolved, so did Ravi's understanding of himself. The couch potato who once doubted his own abilities now stood tall, confident in the knowledge that he possessed skills and strengths he had never fully appreciated. The jungle adventure had been a crucible, burning away his self-doubt and revealing a core of resilience and ingenuity he hadn't known existed.

Ravi found himself reflecting on the journey that had led him to this point. He recalled the initial decision to rescue his brother, a choice that had seemed foolhardy to everyone, including himself. Now, he recognized that moment as the first step in a profound personal transformation. "I never thought I had it in me," Ravi confided to his journal one night. "But out there, in the face of real danger, I discovered a part of myself I never knew existed. It was like all those TV shows had been preparing me for this moment, even though I never realized it."

This newfound self-awareness led Ravi to reassess his goals and aspirations. The young man who had once been content to live vicariously through his television screen now felt a burning desire to experience life firsthand. He began to see his extensive TV knowledge not as a crutch or an escape, but as a foundation upon which to build real-world experiences.

Ravi's family watched with a mixture of surprise and delight as he began to channel his energy into new pursuits. He joined a local hiking club, eager to explore the outdoors he had once only experienced through nature shows. His knowledge of wildlife and survival techniques, honed through years of documentary watching, made him a valuable member of the group. Fellow hikers were often amazed at his ability to identify plants, track animals, and navigate using natural landmarks.

Moreover, Ravi's adventure had sparked an interest in storytelling. He began writing down his experiences, weaving together the drama of the rescue with the lessons he had learned from years of TV watching. His unique perspective – that of a reluctant hero whose seemingly useless hobby had ultimately saved the day – resonated with people. Local schools invited him to speak, and Ravi found that he had a knack for captivating audiences with his tale.

This newfound passion for sharing his story led Ravi to consider a career in media. "Maybe I could create the kind of shows that inspired me," he mused to his family over dinner one evening. "Programs that not only entertain but also teach valuable skills." His parents exchanged glances, still adjusting to this new, ambitious version of their son. But their smiles were genuine as they encouraged him to pursue this dream.

As Ravi explored these new avenues, he also found himself becoming a source of inspiration for others. Young people who had felt similarly directionless or undervalued saw in Ravi a testament to the potential that lies dormant in unexpected places. He received letters from fans who had heard his story, thanking him for showing that even seemingly unproductive hobbies could lead to greatness.

The family dynamic continued to evolve in the weeks following the rescue. Family dinners, once tense affairs filled with pointed comments about Ravi's lack of direction, became lively discussions. Ravi's parents and siblings found themselves genuinely interested in his observations and ideas. His ability to draw parallels between TV shows and real-life situations, once dismissed as trivial, was now appreciated for its creativity and insight.

Even Ravi's viewing habits changed. While he still enjoyed his favorite shows, he now watched with a more critical eye, always looking for practical applications or deeper meanings. He began to see television not as an escape from life, but as a window into diverse experiences and knowledge that could enrich his real-world adventures.

The rescue had also brought about a shift in the family's overall dynamics. They had been forced to confront the reality that they had underestimated and misunderstood Ravi for years. This realization led to more open communication and a conscious effort to appreciate each family member's unique qualities and contributions.

Ravi's mother, in particular, underwent a profound change in her parenting approach. She had always pushed her children towards conventional definitions of success, but Ravi's unconventional heroism made her reconsider these values. "I've learned that there's more than one path to becoming a person of worth," she confided to a friend. "Ravi taught me that sometimes, the things we dismiss as unimportant can be the very things that save us."

As the chapter draws to a close, we see Ravi standing at the threshold of a new chapter in his life. The once-derided couch potato has blossomed into a confident, ambitious young man with a unique perspective on the world. His family, once skeptical of his potential, now stands firmly behind him, eager to see what he will accomplish next.

The rescue mission had not only saved his brother but had also salvaged Ravi's self-esteem and reshaped his family's perceptions. It was a powerful reminder that heroism often emerges from unexpected places, and that the skills and knowledge we accumulate, even from seemingly trivial sources, can prove invaluable in the face of adversity.

As we look ahead to the final chapter of Ravi's tale, we see a young man poised to take on new challenges, armed with the confidence of his jungle adventure and the unwavering support of his family. The couch potato has transformed into a vibrant, engaged individual, ready to make his mark on the world beyond the screen.

Chapter 20: Beyond the Screen

As we transition from the previous chapter, where Ravi reflected on his journey and the family came to terms with his newfound abilities, we now explore how this adventure has fundamentally changed Ravi's outlook on life and his family's perception of him.

The living room, once Ravi's sanctuary of endless television marathons, now felt different. The worn-out couch that had molded to his form over countless hours seemed to beckon less insistently. Ravi found himself spending more time gazing out the window, his mind replaying the vivid experiences of his jungle adventure. The television, still on, now served more as background noise than the focal point of his existence.

Ravi's family, too, viewed the space differently. Where once they saw a lazy, unmotivated young man wasting his potential, they now recognized a hero who had used his unconventional knowledge to save his brother's life. The change in their perception was palpable, evident in the proud glances and the newfound respect in their voices when they spoke to him.

One evening, as Ravi channel-surfed, he paused on a nature documentary. The lush green forests on screen, once merely a backdrop for entertainment, now evoked memories of his own trials and triumphs. He found himself leaning forward, absorbing information with a new intensity, his mind connecting the facts presented with his real-world experiences.

"You know," Ravi's father said, entering the room and noticing his son's engrossment, "I never thought I'd say this, but maybe all that TV watching wasn't such a waste after all." There was a hint of humor in his voice, but the underlying tone of respect was unmistakable.

Ravi turned to his father, a small smile playing on his lips. "It's funny, Dad. I always thought these shows were just an escape from real life. But now, I see them as a window to possibilities I never imagined."

This newfound perspective extended beyond just nature documentaries. Ravi found himself approaching every show with a more critical eye, constantly asking himself how the information or skills presented could be applied in real-life situations. He began keeping a journal, jotting down interesting facts, survival techniques, and problem-solving strategies he encountered in various programs.

However, Ravi's transformation wasn't limited to his TV-watching habits. The confidence gained from his jungle adventure spilled over into other aspects of his life. He started taking short hikes in nearby parks, putting his survival skills to practice in controlled environments. These excursions, while far less dramatic than his rescue mission, gave him a taste of the real-world application of his knowledge and left him hungry for more.

Ravi's brother, still recovering from his ordeal, became an unexpected ally in these new pursuits. Having witnessed firsthand the practical application of Ravi's TV-derived knowledge, he was eager to join his younger brother on these outdoor adventures. Their shared experience had forged a new bond between them, replacing the former dynamic of the successful older sibling and the underachieving younger one with a partnership of equals.

"Remember that time you used the trick from 'MacGyver' to start a fire?" Ravi's brother asked during one of their hikes. "I never thought I'd see the day when your TV obsession would save our lives."

Ravi laughed, remembering the moment. "Neither did I. But you know what? It made me realize that knowledge, no matter where it comes from, has value. It's all about how you use it."

This realization became a guiding principle for Ravi as he navigated his new approach to life. He began to see learning opportunities everywhere, not just on the television screen. He signed up for first aid classes, reasoning that while TV shows had given him a basic understanding, formal training would enhance his skills. He also joined a local hiking club, eager to learn from experienced outdoorsmen and apply his knowledge in group settings.

Ravi's family watched this transformation with a mixture of pride and amazement. His mother, who had once despaired over his seeming lack of direction, now found herself bragging to relatives about her son's adventures and subsequent personal growth.

"It's like he's finally found his calling," she confided to a friend over tea. "Who would have thought that all those hours in front of the TV were preparing him for something like this?"

Indeed, Ravi had found a way to bridge his indoor interests with real-world experiences, creating a balanced lifestyle that surprised even himself. He still enjoyed his TV shows, but now they served as a springboard for real-life adventures and learning experiences rather than an escape from reality.

This new balance extended to his social life as well. Ravi, once content with the company of fictional characters, now found himself eager to share his experiences and newfound knowledge with others. He started a blog chronicling his journey from couch potato to real-life hero, interweaving anecdotes from his rescue mission with tips on applying TV knowledge to everyday situations. To his surprise, the blog gained a following, attracting both outdoor enthusiasts and fellow TV lovers intrigued by his unique perspective.

As Ravi's confidence grew, so did his ambitions. He began to explore career options that would allow him to combine his love for television with his newfound passion for real-world adventures. The idea of becoming a consultant for survival-based reality shows appealed to him, as did the possibility of hosting his own program that bridged the gap between TV knowledge and practical application.

"You've come a long way from the guy who couldn't be bothered to leave the couch," his brother remarked one day, as they discussed Ravi's future plans. "I'm proud of you, little brother."

Ravi's journey had not only changed him but had also transformed his family dynamics. The once-strained relationships, marked by disappointment and misunderstanding, had given way to mutual respect and appreciation. Family dinners, once silent affairs punctuated only by the sound of the TV in the background, were now lively discussions where Ravi shared his latest adventures and the family eagerly contributed their own ideas and experiences.

As Ravi looked to the future, he felt a sense of excitement he had never known before. The world beyond the screen, once intimidating and uninteresting, now beckoned with endless possibilities. He had discovered that life could be as thrilling and rewarding as any TV show, with the added benefit of being real and tangible.

"Life's the ultimate reality show," Ravi often said, "and I'm finally ready to be an active participant."

This sentiment encapsulated Ravi's transformation. He had moved beyond being a passive observer of life through the lens of television to becoming an active participant in his own adventure. The skills and knowledge he had accumulated through years of TV watching had proven to be valuable, but it was the application of this knowledge in real-world situations that had truly changed his life.

As we close this chapter on Ravi's journey, we see a young man poised at the threshold of a new life. The couch potato has evolved into an adventurer, the TV addict into a knowledge seeker. Ravi's story serves as a testament to the power of personal growth and the unexpected ways in which our passions can shape our destinies. It reminds us that sometimes, the most extraordinary journeys begin in the most ordinary of places – even if that place is in front of a television screen.

Book Conclusion

Ravi's journey from couch potato to hero is a testament to the untapped potential that lies within us all. Through his adventure to rescue his brother, Ravi discovered strengths he never knew he possessed, challenging the perceptions of those around him and, most importantly, himself. His clever application of knowledge gleaned from television shows demonstrates that learning can come from unexpected sources, and that wisdom is found not just in traditional education, but in our ability to adapt and apply information creatively.

The transformation of Ravi's family dynamics highlights the importance of looking beyond surface judgments. Initially dismissed as lazy and unambitious, Ravi's courage and resourcefulness in the face of adversity forced his family to reevaluate their preconceptions. This shift in perspective serves as a powerful reminder that people are capable of growth and change, often in ways we least expect.

Ravi's adventure also underscores the value of perseverance and self-belief. Despite initial setbacks and moments of doubt, he consistently found ways to overcome obstacles, drawing on his unique set of skills and knowledge. His journey from self-doubt to self-confidence mirrors the personal growth many of us experience when pushed outside our comfort zones.

Ultimately, "The Lost Tiger" is a story about balance and the integration of different aspects of life. Ravi's experience taught him to appreciate both the virtual world of television and the real-world adventures that await beyond the screen. His newfound approach to life, combining the lessons learned from both realms, points to a future where he can thrive by leveraging his diverse experiences and knowledge. As we close the book on Ravi's extraordinary tale, we are left with a powerful message: within each of us lies a hidden tiger, waiting to be unleashed. By embracing our unique qualities and experiences, we too can rise to meet life's challenges, surprising ourselves and those around us with our hidden strengths and abilities.

138